Maybe Next Summer

I sat absolutely still in my hiding place, afraid even to take a deep breath. I heard nothing else, no other sound. Somebody was out there, though, I knew, and I had to find out who it was and what he was up to. . . . I had just left the cover of a mesquite tree and was making for a clump of creosote bushes when the voice cut through the quiet. "Que pasa?" it said.

The voice shot out again . . . "Alto!" it said, and then in English, "Freeze, buddy!"

Believe me, I froze!

Seventeen-year-old Matt Althaus had never been so scared in his life. There he was, alone in the desert, and he had just been caught by the very men he had been spying on, trying to find out who had been smuggling truckloads of illegal aliens across the Mexican border.

When Matt first arrives in Arizona, a summer spent playing detective is the farthest thing from his mind. Matt wants to learn the newspaper business. So when his father's best friend, Mitch Garrity, invites Matt to spend the summer working on his newspaper, the Crandall *Daily Chronicle*,

Matt accepts with enthusiasm. Matt has wanted to be a journalist as long as he can remember, so a summer working as a reporter is an exciting prospect.

The summer seems even more promising when Matt meets Mitch's daughter, beautiful, blonde Shannon, who also works at the *Chronicle*. It's through Shannon that Matt accidentally stumbles into the illegal smuggling operation, and finds himself working as an investigative reporter a little sooner than he planned.

Matt discovers that journalistic excellence and integrity have their costs as well as their rewards, however, as he discovers some disturbing leads and follows them through to a surprising and painful conclusion.

Maybe Next Summer

by

DON SCHELLIE

FOUR WINDS PRESS
NEW YORK

LIBRARY OF CONGRESS CATALOGING IN PUBLICATION DATA

Schellie, Don.
  Maybe next summer.

  SUMMARY: Working for a small town Arizona
newspaper for the summer, 17-year-old Matt
accidentally stumbles into an operation smuggling
Mexicans across the border.
  [1. Journalism—Fiction. 2. Smuggling—
Fiction. 3. Arizona—Fiction] I. Title.
PZ7.S3433May   [Fic]   79–6338
ISBN 0–590–07585–3

Published by Four Winds Press
A division of Scholastic Magazines, Inc., New York, N.Y.
Copyright © 1980 by Don Schellie
Printed in the United States of America
Library of Congress Catalog Card Number: 79–6338
1 2 3 4 5 84 83 82 81 80

*For
Kristi,
Kendall, and
Leslie,
just because.*

Maybe Next Summer

1

I KEPT WISHING it were a TV cop show and that a commercial about smelly armpits or panty hose would come on the screen the way it always happens just when things are getting exciting and the good guy is in big trouble, but this wasn't a TV show. It was real life and I was the one in trouble and there wouldn't be a commercial about loose false teeth flashing onto the tube to save me. Being smart enough to figure that out, I knew there wasn't anything else I could do to save my skin but fight back, so I did.

It was my own fault, though, being in that spot. I had heard voices over the next hill and thought at last I had found Shannon and her friends. It must've been at least an hour that I had been wandering alone on the desert, first looking for snipe and, after I got wise, looking for the rest of the kids. So when I heard the voices I just lost my head and trotted over the hill, hollering like a second grader at recess time and shining my flashlight every which way.

Only it wasn't Shan and her friends who were making all the noise. It was some men I didn't know and when I popped into their sight they all began pointing at me and talking in Spanish.

During my freshman and sophomore years I had taken Spanish, but mostly I learned things like "My pen is green" and "This is the house of my uncle," and what those men were saying didn't sound like anything in those *Pedro y Maria* dialogues Mrs. Orth had had us translate in our workbooks. Learning as much Spanish as I could and brushing up on the little bit I already knew was something I wanted to do that summer, but this was too much and too soon!

Two of the men had come at me and I didn't know what they had in mind, so I turned tail and headed back over the hill and out of sight. Or so I thought. They were faster than I—at least the smaller guy was—and it wasn't more than a minute before he brought me down with a flying tackle and had a half nelson on me. The big one caught up with us and tried to help his little buddy, but he wasn't much of a fighter. Besides, his friend was doing all right by himself. The small one kept his hold on me and the big one tried to gather up my legs to keep my feet still. That's when I really started fighting back.

I kicked and I twisted and I grunted and got my arms worked loose and then started swinging at them like a windmill, in hopes of doing some damage to those two. Then I butted at them with my head and tried to kick them where it would hurt the most. But I realized they weren't hitting me or kicking me or anything like that. They weren't as interested in fighting me, as they were in merely subduing me. You know, in just holding me still and keeping me away from whatever it was on the other side of the hill—something they didn't want me to see.

Giving a hard twist and jerk with every bit of energy I had, I broke loose, turned and ran off. Only I twisted so fast that I lost my balance and stumbled right into a big jumping cactus—cholla, they're called—and those million needles in my left arm and side made me forget about everything else.

Right away I tried to pick the cactus out of my hide and of course the two guys I was fighting with grabbed me again. They watched for a few seconds and must have seen that I had a bunch of cholla on me because they were awfully careful then about the way they handled me.

They exchanged a few words in fast Spanish and I couldn't make out so much as a *donde* or *esta* or *enchilada* or anything, and then one of them—the big one, it was—reached into his pocket and pulled a gun on me.

The moon was high overhead and it was almost full, so the desert night was silvery bright, but moonlight shadows can play tricks on your eyes. What he pulled out of his pocket looked as much like a gun as anything could have, and I figured that was the end of me. My knees just went weak. As much as I was hurting from those cactus needles, I wasn't quite ready to die. My eyes were just fixed on that gun and I tried to think of some fancy trick I could pull to disarm the guy, but then he moved closer to me and I saw that it wasn't a gun he was holding. It was a *comb!*

If I hadn't been so scared I would have laughed right

out loud. I mean, right in the middle of a fight you don't expect your opponent to pull out his comb and give his hair a few swipes with it. But then I saw that it was *my* hair he intended to comb, because he started coming toward me holding the comb like he meant business.

God, I thought, if all they wanted to do was comb my hair, they didn't have to chase me and put a half nelson on me and push me into the cactus patch and do all that roughhousing. Of course I prefer to comb my own hair, but if they were kinky that way and got their kicks out of combing other guys' hair, why fight it? So I stood still.

That was when the big guy started combing my *arm*—the one that was all stickered with those pincushions of cholla. He ran the comb right along close to my skin and let the teeth of the comb get beneath the hunks of cactus, then he flipped it away from me. It tore at my skin and burned like anything for a few seconds, but then it began to feel better. He went right on down my arm and side with his comb, flipping off several of the little pads of cactus. For a thug, he was a pretty nice guy, helping me like that. And smart, too. I'd never have thought to pull cactus off with a comb. Probably I'd have tried to pull it off with my fingers and got it stuck all over them, too.

As it was, my arm felt like I'd had a thousand tetanus shots from a clumsy school nurse, but then the stinging and burning eased off some. I could tell I still had some of the stickers left in me, but most of them were gone.

"*Gracias*," I said, remembering what Mrs. Orth had taught me, and then I whipped around and tried to run off again. The little guy was too fast for me though, and darned if he didn't lay another half nelson on me. That made a complete, whole nelson he'd thrown on me since I met him.

For maybe half a minute they talked some more in Spanish, and though I still couldn't make out the words, from the way they spoke it sounded as if they weren't sure what to do next. From far away I could hear a car approaching. Maybe I was going to be rescued. Maybe it was some of Shannon's friends coming back to look for me. As it came closer I realized it was a truck I was hearing, and not a car at all. And it sounded as though it stopped on the other side of the hill, where I had seen all those people. I wasn't about to be rescued, after all.

Again I tried to pull loose but the little guy just tightened his hold on me. He was strong; his grip was like steel. He said something to his big partner and the big one said, "*Si*," and ran off toward the hill. Before I knew it the man who was holding me threw me to the ground and knelt on my back, pushing my face into the ground.

From beyond that rise I could hear plenty of excited talk in Spanish again, and there was the sound of a truck door squeaking open and then a lot of scrambling, and some hollow thudding noises. A shrill whistle, like a signal, sounded, and the guy on my back grunted. He pushed my face harder into the ground and said something that sounded like, "*Amigo*, stay!"

All at once he was up and running toward that hill. I stayed. I had dirt in my mouth and eyes and I spit and brushed carefully at my eyes and then I managed to stand up and take inventory of myself. I really didn't seem to be hurt, except for all those cactus spines. In the morning I'd probably be bruised and sore all over, but I'd worry about that then. Some thin clouds had moved over the moon and cut down considerably on the light, but I could still make out the figure of my half-nelson friend as he disappeared over the hill. I started off after him, but very slowly, because I didn't want to tangle with any more cactus—or thugs, however considerate— that night.

As I trotted I could hear that same truck door being closed and then locked, and then there was a grinding of gears that sounded as though the driver had a lot of trouble getting it into low, and the grating noise about set my teeth on edge. Then came the sound of the truck moving away slowly and finally roaring off into the night. By the time I reached the top of the rise there was nothing to see, except a shadowy something that may or may not have been a truck, moving away in the distance.

I took it easy going down the hill and when I got to where the people had been waiting all I could make out in the faint light were some scuffle marks and footprints and rutted tire tracks on the soft, sandy desert. I tried to figure out who those people were and what they might've been up to, but I couldn't come up with any answers. Rustlers, maybe. But rustlers rustle cattle, not people, and besides, I never knew any cows that spoke Spanish.

It was about then, with my mouth and eyes still gritty with desert, that I decided that if this was the sort of thing they did for entertainment in Arizona, I was sure as anything going to limit my social life that summer.

The moon was completely clouded over and it started thundering and there were some bolts of lightning that came out of the sky and scared the daylights out of me, so I began walking and presently came to a narrow, unpaved road. There was no way I could tell which direction led to town or to a road that might take me to town. I was as lost as anyone could ever be, so for no good reason at all, I turned to the left and followed the road in that direction.

It wasn't long before the rain came. Welcome to Arizona.

2

NOWHERE IN any of the journalism books I had been reading since I was twelve or thirteen did it say anything about how you might be attacked by unknown assailants or get pushed into cactus or be forced belly-down on the ground with some guy's knee in your back and half of Arizona in your mouth, but it had all happened to me. Maybe that's the price you have to pay when you're an investigative reporter, like me.

Only I wasn't really an investigative reporter. Not yet, at least. In fact I had just arrived in town that afternoon and hadn't so much as laid eyes on the office of the Crandall *Chronicle* yet, so of course I hadn't even written my first news story for the paper. So I couldn't really call myself a *regular* reporter yet, let alone an *investigative* one. Now I was beginning to have doubts. I was almost convinced I should forget my great summer plans and go back home.

Being in that predicament was my own fault, I realized as I sludged along in the rain, soaking wet, my arm and side still stinging from the cactus, and the rest of me sore and aching in eighty places from being held and kneed and thrown to the ground. It was my own fault; I had no one to blame but myself.

After all, I'm seventeen and I think I've got a pretty good head on my shoulders, but after the way I fell for their big joke, I had to admit that "gullible" is my middle name.

Me, I'm Matt Gullible Althaus, Boy Investigative Reporter.

Being a city kid I had never heard of snipe or of snipe hunting or anything of the sort, so how was I to know that snipe hunting was a big joke on yours truly, the original, A-Number-One-All-Time-Champion-Dummy?

Which is how it happened that Shannon and her friends took me snipe hunting that Sunday night, and of course that's where it all started. Not that I blame them, because I was the perfect sucker, just waiting to be given a lick or two. They had no idea what was going to happen to me then, any more than I did.

Maybe we just don't have any snipe around where I live, or at least I hadn't heard anybody mention them. There are plenty of snipe, or snipes or whatever the plural is, in Arizona though, especially around Crandall, which is down on the Mexican border in Papago County, not too many miles west of the New Mexico state line.

As I said, I had arrived in town that day, having gone down there to spend the summer working for my Uncle Mitch Garrity, who is editor and general manager of the *Chronicle*. Shannon is Aunt Beth and Uncle Mitch's daughter, only she isn't really my cousin because Mitch and Beth aren't really my uncle and aunt. Don't worry if that sounds confusing, because I'll explain it later.

Mitch had driven up to Tucson to meet me at the airport and after we got down to Crandall we left my things at the Railroad Hotel, where I'd be living that summer, and then drove over to the Garritys' house for dinner. It had been a long time since I had seen Shannon. The last time was that Thanksgiving our two families spent together at our place when she was eight and I was nine and I hated her guts. We had an awful time. It wasn't that she was spoiled or a brat or anything like that. It's just that she was a pesky girl and I didn't have much use for girls. I've changed since I was nine.

When we arrived at the Garritys' and Shan opened the door to let us in, I knew I didn't hate her anymore. A guy just can't hate a girl who looks that great. Shan is tall and I like tall girls and she has long hair that is about three shades of blonde, but it looks like it got that way from being in the sun a lot, and not from a bottle. Her face is sort of freckly, but on her the freckles look good, and her eyes are large and smokey gray and full of mischief. As we stepped inside she gave her father a kiss and then she shook my hand. I felt cheated.

Shan took a couple of steps back and frowned and bit her lip, studying me. I studied her right back.

"Do they still call you Winky?" she asked. I could feel my ears getting red.

"No," I said, and then I laughed a little bit because I couldn't think of anything to say right away. Finally I said, "Nobody's called me that for years. Guess I've outgrown it. I hope so, at least."

It was hard taking my eyes off Shan, but I grabbed a quick look around and was happy with what I saw. You

can sort of tell what kind of people live in a home, just by
the furniture and things they have around. The Garritys
had old, but nice-looking furniture—a lot of the pieces
were antiques—and there were shelves full of books and
a table with magazines on it. On the floor were Indian
rugs and there were Indian baskets fastened high on the
walls, along with some nice paintings and prints. On the
big, round coffee table there was a bowl of fresh flowers.
Sweet peas, I think. The living room was neat, yet it
looked as though people used it. It was a comfortable
room, just as the Garritys are comfortable people.

Just then Aunt Beth came hurrying out of the kitchen
and she came right up to me and hugged me and gave me
a kiss. Usually I don't go for that sort of thing, but I
really like Beth, so I didn't try to pull away. She was
even prettier than I had remembered her. She looked
exactly like Shannon, except that her hair had a slight
reddish look to it, and she was a few pounds heavier, and
of course, older. I remembered hearing that she came
from a rich, old ranching family, and that she and Mitch
had met when they both were students at the University
of New Mexico.

"Winky!" she said, stepping back to look at me. "Why,
I'd never have recognized you!"

"It's *Matt*," said Mitch. "You can't call a kid *that* big,
Winky!" We all laughed.

"I'll try to remember," Shannon teased, "but Winky's
all I've ever called you. You'll just have to forgive me if I
forget and call you that sometimes."

She was so beautiful she could call me anything, I
thought, just so she called me. But I didn't say that.

What I said was, "You do and you'll wish you hadn't!" I frowned and tried to look mean.

"You don't scare *me*," she said, and she turned and walked into the kitchen.

During dinner they asked all sorts of questions about my family. The usual things. They wanted to know how my folks were and was everybody well and was my Dad getting fat and how was the accounting business and who did Allison look like (Allison's my kid sister) and things like that. I hoped I didn't tell them more about my folks than they really wanted to know, but they kept asking all those questions, so they must've been interested. My Dad and Mitch had been awfully close during the war in Korea, and even though they lived half a country apart now, they kept up. They corresponded regularly and talked on the telephone once in a while. I've always felt very close to Mitch, because if it hadn't been for him, I wouldn't be writing this. In fact, I just wouldn't *be*, period. My middle name is Garrity, which shows you how much my folks think of Uncle Mitch.

A thousand times Dad has told me the story about how Mitch saved his life in Korea. I won't go into all the details of it now because it takes Dad about a half hour to tell it, but they were separated from their patrol and were pinned down by enemy fire along some river not long after the Red Chinese got into the war. Dad was hit badly in the leg and was bleeding a lot. The Communists started moving in on them, and Mitch picked up Dad and ran with him—literally *ran* with him, and my Dad's better than six feet tall—for about a hundred yards to where they found the rest of their patrol. The unit medic stopped Dad's bleeding, and the surgeons later saved the leg, which was really mangled. That run was amazing, Dad says, because the Communists kept up a steady fire the whole time Mitch was running. Dad always says it was a miracle that they didn't get hit. "I owe him one," he says every time he tells me the story. "Your Uncle Mitch saved my life."

So this is one reason I've always thought so much of Mitch, and besides, he and Beth are great people, and Shannon, now that she's grown up, is pretty neat herself. Even though I hadn't seen them for years, I felt just as easy and comfortable with them as I do with my own family. In some ways, more.

For a long time after we finished eating we sat at the table and talked and did a lot of laughing and then the doorbell rang. It was some of Shannon's friends, invited over to meet me. We volunteered to do the dishes but Mitch said he and Beth would get things cleared up in no time, so Shan and I went out into the patio with her friends. The sun was down and it was still hot, but nobody else seemed to mind so I didn't complain. We sat around for about an hour just talking and listening to records and drinking anything cold and wet that we could find in the Garrity refrigerator.

Everybody was talking about Crandall High School—you know, about other kids and teachers and who was going with who—and then one of the guys mentioned snipe hunting. It was the one named Pete, I think.

"A night like this makes me think of snipe," he said. "I haven't been snipe hunting for a long time."

"What's a snipe?" I asked. That's where I went wrong.

One thing led to another and before I knew it, we were piling into a car and heading out into the boondocks so I could learn all the finer points of hunting snipe. I didn't want to seem pushy, but I got in next to Shannon because she was the only one in the crowd I really knew, and, besides, if I had my way we'd get to be awfully good friends that summer, so why not start now?

We drove for probably a couple of miles on some back roads that seemed to take us due west of town, although later I was convinced that we must've gone at least a couple of *hundred* miles. Along a lonely stretch of road we parked the car and all of us climbed out. The moon was big so we could see pretty well out there. It was really nice of those kids, I thought. Here I was, a total stranger, and they were going to all that trouble to teach me how to hunt snipe. Western hospitality, you might call it. I could tell right then that it was going to be a great summer if everybody I met in Crandall was as nice as Shannon's friends were. When we were out of the car she handed me a folded-up cloth.

"What's that?" I asked her.

"A pillowcase," she told me.

"So what's a pillowcase for? Are we camping?" I chuckled, thinking I'd throw in a little bit of big-city humor.

Ernesto, who had graduated in June, said, "No, you use the pillowcase to catch the snipe in."

"That's right," said the tall boy they called Buck. "You hold this flashlight and that'll attract the snipe. In the meantime we'll all be beating the bushes off in the distance, sending the birds your way. They'll zero in on your light beam and as they run toward it, you grab 'em in the pillowcase."

"It's as easy as that? You mean they'll just come running right to me?"

"That's all there is to it," said Sandy, who wore glasses. "But you have to make sure you hold the pillowcase wide open or the snipe will run right past it."

If that's all there is to snipe hunting, it's a cinch, I thought. Even though I was a city kid, I figured I had the hang of it. I'd show them a thing or two about hunting snipe. Then, all of a sudden, Buck hollered that he spied one. He pulled off his big cowboy hat—he lived on a ranch and wore boots and Levi's and a wide-brimmed hat and all—and made a dive with it toward a bush.

"Got one!" he yelled, and we all crowded around for a look. As I got close he lifted his hat slightly from the ground, then yelped and flung up his arms and swore. "That little critter bit me on the finger and got away!" he said. And then Buck poked the injured finger into his mouth and sucked it like it was a popsicle.

"Did it draw blood?" Shan asked. She sounded concerned.

"Just a bad pinch," he mumbled around his finger, and put his hat back on his head. I never did see that snipe.

One of the other fellows pointed off toward a clump of cactus and said he saw one dart into it. I got up close and shined the flashlight into the patch, but didn't see that one, either. Those snipes were about as speedy as anything alive, that was for sure. I was beginning to see where maybe snipe hunting wasn't as easy as I had first thought it would be, and it seemed dangerous, too.

"Watch it, Matt!" The warning came from the little girl whose name was Maria. "There's one coming your way!" Quickly I got down on my knees and held the pillowcase wide open with the flashlight behind it, but I missed the snipe. Pete told me it ran right past my leg. Darned if I could see it, though. They're very fast.

"Oh, I wish you'd caught that one," Shannon said. "It was big—*real* big!" I felt bad about it, too.

Then the blond boy, Pete, darted off into some bushes. Before long he came out again, swearing like anything. The back of his shirt was ripped and he sounded as though he was hurting. A couple of big snipe had jumped him in the underbrush, he said, and had given him a tough time, but he had managed to fight them off. I was really sorry that had happened to Pete, since he had been so nice about suggesting that we go snipe hunting. I began to worry, too. Those snipes—they're a lot fiercer than I had imagined birds could be.

"We ain't doing any good here," Buck said. "Come on, maybe we'd all better head over the hill and flush them over here toward Matt."

The idea didn't sound all that great to me, but I didn't want to let on that I was scared. "Okay," I told them, "send those snipes on over. I'm ready for 'em!"

So the others disappeared over the hill, saying they'd form a straight line in the desert and scare them my way. I squatted down, and tucking the flashlight under one arm, held the pillowcase wide open between my hands. Let 'em come, I thought. I was as set to catch snipes as I'd ever be.

For a while I heard the other kids making noises and beating the bushes with sticks and calling out, but their voices got farther and farther away, and after a while it got awfully quiet beyond that hill. I stayed ready though, holding that pillowcase wide open the way they had taught me, just waiting for those snipes.

3

IT MUST'VE BEEN a good fifteen minutes that I had been squatting there, and my legs began to cramp. I stood up and stretched and walked around some, then went back to my post. I guessed the others were having trouble scaring up more snipe, but I stayed with it because I didn't want to disappoint them by missing any birds they sent my way. After about ten more minutes I began to really worry about them. Maybe they were all lost out there on the desert. Maybe they were in trouble. And it was all my fault because I was the guest of honor on the hunt. If I hadn't been so new to town they wouldn't have bothered trying to make me feel like one of the gang and wouldn't have brought me out there and got lost or into trouble or whatever it was that was keeping them. I felt responsible. So I squatted there, worrying about them.

And I worried about myself, too. It was getting late and I had a lot to do before I went to bed and I wanted to get a good night's sleep so I'd be fresh in the morning for my first day on the job. I didn't want to blow it.

Mitch was nice enough to hire me for the summer and

that meant a lot to me and I didn't want to disappoint him. In April my Dad had called him and told him about how interested I am in journalism, and how I wanted to major in it at Northwestern University—that's where the Medill School of Journalism is—and did he have any advice?

Not a week later I had a long letter from Mitch telling me the important thing was to work on the high school paper (I'd been on the staff since I was a freshman) and to take all the journalism and composition classes I could in high school. He said it was a good idea for me to take lots of social studies and sciences, too, so I'd know a little bit about a lot of things. Well, I'd been doing all that anyway, and I'd read just about every book on journalism and newspapers and newspaper people that I could put my hands on, but it was nice to hear from Mitch that I'd been doing all the right things.

In May he phoned us from Arizona. He was going to have a temporary vacancy on the staff through the summer and did I want to work for the Crandall *Chronicle* for a few months?

Of course I wouldn't get rich in those two months— nobody gets rich in the newspaper business, anyway— but the *Chronicle* would pay my air fare and would pay me enough to cover room and board and have a few dollars left for spending money. Mom and Dad talked it over that night and I knew there was a lot going for me. Aunt Beth would see to it that I had a home-cooked meal a few times a week and Mitch would be right there to keep an eye on me. Parents worry about things like that. And maybe I'd get the idea of being a reporter out of my system. I knew Dad hoped I would. He was determined that I'd major in accounting in college and then join his firm. I was determined that I wouldn't. I was about as much interested in being an accountant as I was in being an organ grinder's monkey.

They decided to let me go, and the last few weeks of school before summer vacation dragged by slowly. I got a long letter from Mitch telling me not to expect too much. The Crandall *Chronicle*, he said, was not the New York *Times*. Or even the Chicago *Tribune* or the Kansas City *Star*, for that matter.

The *Chronicle* was published six days a week and had a three-man staff, including himself. "You'll be writing everything," he said in the letter, "from police and fire news to church news, sports, weddings and social notes. You'll be covering potluck suppers and softball tournaments and school board meetings and luncheon club speeches. If experience is what you're after, Matt, you'll get plenty of it this summer."

Mitch said I'd be filling in for a young reporter who had just been out of college for a year, who wanted to spend two months bicycling through Europe with his new bride. "So it will work out perfectly for all concerned," he wrote. "You'll get your taste of newspaper life and Larry Gates will have his job waiting for him when he gets back from Europe. He was afraid we might have to replace him permanently."

It was the last paragraph of his letter that really got me excited. "You might be interested to know," it said, "that the other man you'll be working with is Trevor

Brannigan. Maybe you've heard of him. Bran and I will look forward to having you with us this summer. . . ."

Heard of him! Trevor Brannigan was one of my idols. I'd read both of his books. During World War II he had been a famous war correspondent for one of the wire services. His dispatches from Europe and later the South Pacific had been classics. After the war he had a book published of the best of his news stories and I'd read that book at least three times. A lot of people said he was even better than Ernie Pyle. Then he wrote a book of his experiences covering the war and it really goes into how he operated as a correspondent. I learned plenty from that book. There are a lot of photos of him in it, showing him at the front, riding in jeeps and sitting in a foxhole with his portable typewriter on his knees, and another one of him drinking wine with other correspondents. It's one of my favorite books; I was lucky enough to find a copy of it in a used book store. I was really excited. Not only would I be meeting one of my heroes, but I'd be *working* with him, as well! I wondered how such a famous newspaperman happened to be working on the *Chronicle*, but I'd find out soon enough. At least once a day I pulled out Mitch's letter to reread during those long weeks before school ended. I was convinced that I was about the luckiest guy in the world.

Only hunkering there in the desert waiting for Shannon and her buddies to chase the snipes my way, I wasn't feeling at all excited. Or lucky. After a while it began to dawn on me that maybe snipe hunting was a big put-on, a big joke, and the joke was on me. The longer I waited the more I felt that way. That's when this big chump decided to try to find the others if they were still around, and if I couldn't find them, then walk back toward town. The way things were going, I'd be in great shape when I showed up in the *Chronicle* office my first day on the job.

So I started wandering around the desert and that's when I heard those voices beyond that hill and had my fight with those two men and the run-in with the cactus and got my arm combed. Anyway, finally I found that road and started walking along it not knowing whether it would take me to Crandall or anyplace for that matter, and then it started raining and I got to thinking maybe I wouldn't last through two months of newspaper work. I hadn't been in Arizona more than a few hours and already I'd had more bad things happen to me than had happened to me in the whole last year at home. Five years.

And Shannon. I hated her again. Maybe the snipe hunt wasn't her idea, but she went along with it. I could just hear her and her friends laughing about the stupe from the big city back East who fell for the old snipe-hunting bit. Ha, ha, ha. Big joke. I could hardly wait to get my hands on Shannon. I didn't have long to wait, as it turned out.

The rain was heavy but there was no shelter nearby that I could see. It was thundering and the lightning was zapping all around and I was really getting scared. Later I learned that it was just an average Arizona summer electrical storm, but it had me plenty worried. There were dips in the unpaved road where the water ran across—washes, they call them—as much as a couple of feet deep. Not knowing any better I just kept splashing along, sloshing right through them. I knew I couldn't get any wetter than I already was.

Looking back over my shoulder I saw some far-off headlights coming toward me, all dim and fuzzy through the rain. I didn't know what to do. I was afraid that it might be those people in the truck, and that the two guys I had fought with were coming back to finish their job. Maybe comb my other arm. But then again, maybe it wasn't them. Maybe it was Pete or Ernesto or one of Shannon's other friends feeling guilty about leaving me out there in the desert. So when the headlights got close I waved my arms like a maniac and flagged down the car. It was a yellow Chevy station wagon, like the one Mitch had driven when he picked me up that afternoon in Tucson. It stopped right beside me and the driver leaned over and opened the passenger door. When the dome light came on I could see that the driver was Shannon.

"I usually don't pick up hitchhikers," she said as I climbed into the car. I didn't answer. I just slammed the door. Hard.

"Oh, Matt," she said as I settled in. "I'm sorry."

"I'll bet you are," I told her.

"But I am! I had no idea you'd be out there this long and that we'd have a storm."

"You haven't heard the half of it," I said. "I got into a fight."

"Who on earth did you find to fight with out there?"

"I didn't find them—they found me."

She made a long, drawn-out "Ohhhh" sound, and before I could stop her Shannon reached over and patted my arm.

I yelped. "And I tangled with a cactus, too," I said, clenching my teeth. She had patted me right on all those stickers.

"Oh, Matt," she said again, and it really sounded as though she was sorry. Shan leaned over and kissed me on the cheek. That didn't help my aches and pains and pride, but it didn't hurt them, either. I quit hating her again. Shannon isn't the kind of girl you can hate for long.

She made a U-turn—I had been walking in the wrong direction—and headed back toward town. As she drove I told her all about what had happened to me. She kept telling me how sorry she was.

"Who do you suppose they were?" I asked her. "And what were they doing out there in the middle of the night?"

"I have no idea," Shan said. "There's a lot of narcotics smuggling going on down here along the border. Mostly marijuana and heroin, but those people, I imagine, don't go around making a lot of noise. And I hear they mostly use airplanes these days."

"Were we close to the border?"

"When we left you you were about a quarter mile from Mexico. It could have been illegal aliens, too. A lot of Mexican people who can't get permission to immigrate into the United States legally just jump the fence or slit it and sneak into this country. And there are some people who make a business of smuggling the aliens into the U.S., too."

"Well, I sure don't know who it was out there, but one thing's certain," I said, "whatever it was they were up to, they didn't want me to see it."

For a while neither of us said anything. I was thinking about all that had happened to me that night and I imagine Shannon was busy concentrating on the driving. The rain was still coming down and it was like driving through Niagara Falls, but Shan handled the wagon like a real pro. Sometimes I get nervous the way other people drive, but I wasn't at all edgy with her at the wheel. As we got into town Shan broke the silence.

"Maybe we'd better stop at the sheriff's office so you can report what happened," she suggested.

"We can't do that," I said. "I don't even want to tell your folks about it. If it got back to my parents they'd get worried and have me on a plane headed for home before any of us knew what happened, and I don't even have my bags unpacked yet. They worry a lot."

"Then what should I tell my folks?"

"That you all took me snipe hunting and I got lost and fell down a couple of times and that I tangled with a cactus. That'll be the truth, just not the whole story."

"I hate not being completely honest with them," Shannon said. "We have a real good relationship. And they'd want to know about what happened to you."

"Yeah, but if it means my leaving here before I even see the *Chronicle* office, it'll ruin the whole summer. And besides, one of the guys I fought with called me

'*amigo*,' and doesn't that mean 'friend'? At least that's
what it sounded like. How about it, Shannon? After that
snipe-hunt thing, don't you think you owe me a favor?"

"You win," she said. "We'll keep it a secret between
us, but I do want to take you home and get those cactus
stickers out of you before they start festering. They can
be nasty."

So we went to her house. Aunt Beth and Uncle Mitch
were still up, so everybody got into the act. I stripped
down to my waist and they all yanked stickers out of my
arm and side with tweezers and Scotch Tape and long
fingernails and then we had sandwiches and milk. It was
almost like a party, except that I didn't enjoy being the
entertainment. They must've pulled a hundred tiny
stickers from my hide. Her parents weren't very happy
with Shannon for taking me on the snipe hunt, but I
laughed about it and told them it was my own fault. I
told them that I got a big kick out of it—a lot of laughs. I
don't think they believed me.

It was late when Shannon drove me to the Railroad
Hotel. The rain had stopped and the night was cool and
fresh smelling.

"You'd better hurry up and sleep fast," she told me as
we pulled up in front of the hotel. "I'll bet you'll have a
busy day tomorrow."

"Bet it won't be half as busy as this night was," I said.
"At least I hope it won't. I don't think I've ever had a
busier one." We laughed. Then she told me she'd see me
in the morning.

"You coming down to visit me?" I asked.

"No, I work in the *Chronicle* business office—full time

in the summer. I take classified ads and type letters and sell subscriptions and answer the phone—I do just about everything."

I told her I was glad I'd be seeing her every day and then I thanked her for the ride home and started to open the door.

She reached out and touched my arm. This time she was careful not to touch me where the stickers had been. "About the snipe hunt—I'm sorry, I really am." Then she smiled and added, "And I'm glad you're here, Winky. It'll be a great summer for us."

I told her good night and got out of the car and watched as she drove off. When she was out of sight I climbed the stairs to the front porch of the old hotel. Tired as I was, it felt almost like my feet were floating on air.

If only she wouldn't call me Winky.

4

MY HERO WAS old and fat and almost bald and he was grouchy as a bear. I was shattered.

Of course I should have realized Trevor Brannigan wouldn't look like those pictures of him in his book, because after all, they were taken back in the 1940s and you know how long ago that was. Now he must be in his sixties. At least he looks that old. I guess I had expected too much.

Maybe I'd thought he'd even be wearing his war correspondent's uniform with the black-and-yellow shoulder patch on it, and that he'd have a lock of his wavy hair falling down over his forehead like in the picture of him with Ernest Hemingway taken in Paris the day it was liberated from the Nazis. They're all smiles in that picture, holding bottles of French wine and surrounded by a bunch of pretty mademoiselles.

Instead of wavy hair, the Trevor Brannigan I met had a shaggy fringe of gray around his balding head, and instead of a uniform he wore a pair of wash pants and scuffed loafers and over his sport shirt, an old gray-brown sweater that buttoned up the front. Here I was dying from that famous Arizona heat, and he was wearing a sweater.

Mitch introduced us and Bran looked up from his typewriter and gave me a hard look from head to toe. I felt like I was a beef roast in the butcher shop and he was the customer trying to decide whether or not I was worth buying. Then, with his left hand he took an unlit cigar from his mouth and stuck his right hand out for me to shake. He lifted one bristly eyebrow as we shook hands and looked me straight in the eye. "What's wrong with marine biology, Matt?" he asked me.

I didn't understand what he meant. "What did you say?" I asked. Mitch chuckled. Bran went on. "Marine biology—why don't you go into marine biology or nuclear physics or something like that? Anything but journalism." I could feel my face getting red.

"But being a reporter's all I've ever wanted to do," I told him. He shook his head.

"One of those, eh," he mumbled, almost to himself. Then he said, "Nice-looking kid like you should think twice. This is a lousy business. It wears you down, it makes you old before your time and sick and. . . ."

Mitch laughed again. "Go easy on the boy, Bran," he said. "You know you wouldn't trade newspapering for anything." Bran grunted, jammed his cigar into his mouth and went back to his typing. Except when he ate, I discovered, Trevor Brannigan always had an unlit cigar in his mouth. "Don't mind Bran," Mitch said to me then. Only he said it loud enough so Bran would be sure to hear it, too. "He tries to seem rough and tough on the outside, but he's really a sweetheart. Inside he's just a big marshmallow." Well, he sure had me fooled, I thought.

Mitch said he'd introduce me later to everybody else in the building, "but right now we've got to see about getting a paper put together."

The newsroom wasn't much to get excited about. Like Bran, it wasn't at all what I had expected. It was on the second floor of a two-story brick building on a side street just off Copper Avenue, which was Crandall's main street. On the first floor was the business office, where Shan worked. You entered through the front door into a little lobby area, and behind a large counter the circulation and advertising and business office people had their desks. Out behind the business office was a ground-floor addition to the building, and that's where the press and Linotype machines and all the other printing equipment were located. Everybody just called that area the "back shop." At the end of the business office counter was a swinging gate, and to get to the newsroom you went through that gate, turned left and climbed a narrow flight of stairs to the second floor.

Our living room at home is larger than the *Chronicle*'s newsroom, and a thousand times less cluttered. In the center of the room two big desks were pushed together, back to back. Uncle Mitch sat at one and Bran at the other. My desk was one of two against the back wall. Nobody really used that other desk. It was just a spare, and things that nobody knew what to do with got piled on it.

Against another wall was a large oak table, and it was

stacked high with newspapers from other towns around
the state. On the counter next to it were a couple of
months of back issues of the *Chronicle*. In a small alcove
behind Mitch's desk was the Associated Press teletype
machine, which clattered out news of what was happening elsewhere in Arizona and the rest of the world. Next
to the teletype was a machine that turned photos into
thin plastic engravings so we could run pictures in the
paper. I won't try to explain how it worked because I
never really learned how myself. It was just there and
either Bran or Mitch usually operated it.

On the walls were maps of Papago County, Arizona
and the United States and a big one of the world; some
front pages of the *Chronicle* were taped up here and
there, though I don't know why. There were memos and
notes tacked up, too, most of them yellow and dusty,
looking as though they'd been hanging there since
Arizona became a state in 1912. At the rear of the
newsroom was a doorway leading to a hall. The bathroom was back there, and so were the storeroom and
Uncle Mitch's private office, which he hardly ever used.

The whole place was dusty and dirty. No two pieces
of furniture matched. Some of them had been painted a
deep red sometime in the past, and other pieces had been
painted green; still others were varnished oak, and all of
them were chipped and scratched. The floor was tile and
it got swept once a week, whether it needed it or not,
and once a month it was mopped. Around the room were
three or four big wastebaskets that somehow managed
to get filled every day and emptied every night. Beside

each desk was an old typewriter table holding an even older typewriter. My Underwood looked like Civil War surplus.

Larry Gates, the young reporter who was bicycling in Europe, had cleaned out a couple of drawers of his desk for me to use, and cleared everything off the top of it. It was the only uncluttered flat surface in the whole newsroom, the floor included. I found a cloth, dusted the top of the desk, wiped the chair and then blew the dust from the typewriter. I was in business.

Those first few days I hardly left the office except at lunchtime and after work. Just about all I did was rewrite press releases from government agencies, the universities up in Tucson, Tempe and Flagstaff, big companies with stores or offices in our circulation area, local clubs and churches, and things like that.

During those first days and for as long as I worked on the paper that summer, I wrote a lot of items for the Social Notes column, too, mostly about who had house guests, who celebrated a birthday, and who drove to Phoenix to visit relatives. As you can imagine, it was really exciting, but Mitch said it was a good place for me to begin. He said I'd learn fast the way they did things on the *Chronicle*.

"The Baptist church is having a chicken dinner next week," he'd tell me, handing me a handwritten note from the publicity chairman of the Baptist women's circle. "Give me two or three grafs on it."

"Graf," I learned, means paragraph. So I'd read the note and pick out the most thrilling facts about the chicken dinner and put them in the first, or lead,

paragraph, as it's called. Then I'd follow with the rest of
the information in the next graf or two.

Those first few days I must have written two hundred
news stories, if you can call a chicken dinner news. I
wasn't crazy about it, but Mitch kept saying it was the
fastest way for me to learn what was going on.

Every afternoon, after the *Chronicle* had gone to
press and we had begun to work on the next day's paper,
he would have me pull up a chair beside his desk and
we'd go over the stories I had written.

During those sessions Mitch would take a big soft lead
pencil and mark through a story, editing it as I watched,
telling me what was wrong, but also what was right. He
showed me how to improve my stories by juggling
sentences and paragraphs around, adding words here,
leaving them out there. He talked about getting the
important facts into the first paragraph or two, keeping
sentences and paragraphs short, and using simple
words. He was patient as anything, and I must've
learned more from him those few days than I did my
whole first semester in Journalism I.

One afternoon we walked down to the Crandall Drug
Store for milk shakes and while we drank them, Mitch
lectured me on how important it was to be accurate in
names and addresses and ages and things like that, as
well as in the matter of basic facts.

"We want the people who buy the *Chronicle* to know
that they can believe what we print," he told me. "With
us—with any good newspaper—accuracy and truth must
come first. Even if the truth hurts, we owe it to our
readers to print it. If one of our biggest advertisers is

arrested for drunk driving, for instance, we're obligated to print the story—as we would do with anyone else— even if he threatens to stop advertising with us if we do."

Then Mitch said he'd lectured enough for one after-noon and asked if I had any questions or problems. I shrugged and told him I didn't really have any problems. "But do you think I'll be getting out of the office one of these days to work on some stories?"

"I think you're about ready," he said, his face breaking into an understanding grin.

He wanted to know then if I had any questions to ask or anything to talk over with him and I said no, although I really did want to tell him about my snipe-hunting adventure and ask him who he thought it was I had tangled with, but I decided it would only worry him and maybe get me aboard a plane headed home. So instead I asked Mitch if Trevor Brannigan was always as grumpy as he had been since I showed up that first morning in the *Chronicle* newsroom.

Mitch smiled. He has the kind of smile that could defrost your mother's freezer in two minutes. "That's just Bran's way," he said. "Don't let it get to you, Matt. I think if he were all sweetness and light we'd have to worry. It's a defense mechanism with him. Bran values his privacy and he has the idea that by acting the way he does he can keep people at arm's length. He isn't fooling anyone—especially not himself. He retired from the wire service and settled here in Crandall because he figured it was about as far away from the rat race as he could get. Swore he'd never again set foot inside a newspaper office. In two weeks he came to see me, looking for work.

Not that he needs the money—he's all alone, gets a good pension, has a bundle in the bank—but he just couldn't sit still.

"Bran loves this business, Matt, and he's one of the few real pros I've had the pleasure of knowing. He can't stay away from it. Keep an eye on him, listen to him and you'll learn plenty this summer. Just don't let the gruffness bother you. Trevor Brannigan is all bark and no bite."

"I'm glad to hear that because I had really looked forward to working with him, but he just seems to be so grouchy. . . ." 2117214

"He'll warm up, Matt, and I imagine it'll be soon. Takes him a day or two to take the measure of someone. Just let him see that you're really interested in newspaper work and that you have some talent and he'll take you under his wing and you'll learn more than I or any journ instructor could ever teach you. Give it a few days, Matt."

Mitch asked how my Spanish was coming along. The question took me by surprise, and for a second I chewed at my lip before I remembered.

"*Asi asi,*" I answered, which means, "so-so."

"*Bueno,*" Mitch said. *Bueno* I understood without even having to ask him what it meant, or look it up in my pocket Spanish-English dictionary.

Then he wanted to know if I was settled in at the Railroad Hotel and if my room was all right and everything. "I know it's no palace," he said, "but it's respectable and fairly clean and close to the office, and more important, it's cheap." I told him the room was just fine, though I have to admit it was a white lie, because the room was as dismal and depressing as any I had ever slept in. But I didn't expect to spend much time there, anyway, so I didn't complain. And it was just a block and a half from the *Chronicle* building and only a half block from Copper Avenue and Lincoln Street, which was the busiest intersection in town, and just two blocks from the city building, where the police and fire stations were, so at the Railroad Hotel, I was right in the middle of things.

Mitch paid for our shakes and we walked back toward the office. I'm pretty good sized—almost six feet—but walking next to Mitch, I felt like a shrimp. He must be half a head taller than I am and he's lean and square and has a deep tan. His hair is steel gray and curly and he's about as handsome as any man I've ever known, but in a rugged, outdoorsy way. I'll bet he could have been an actor in Westerns, if he had gone in for that sort of thing. It seemed as though he knew just about everybody in town and they all seemed to like him. As we walked along Copper, people we passed on the street told him hello, a guy in a pickup truck honked his horn at him and waved, and the man who runs the men's clothing store came out to greet him. He introduced me to a few people we met, but didn't say I was an old war buddy's kid who he was doing a favor for, or anything like that. "George," he said to the clothing store man, "I'd like you to meet Matt Althaus—new reporter on the *Chronicle*. I'd appreciate any help you can give him." He made me feel like I belonged, like I was part of the staff, and not just a kid getting a taste of newspaper work for the summer.

When we got to the office door, Mitch stopped and told me he had some stories to check out and some business across the line in La Pizca, and that he'd see me in the morning.

"Be sure you wear your walking shoes, Matt," he said. "We'll be covering a lot of ground."

"I'm really looking forward to it, Uncle Mitch," I said. He wrinkled up his face in a grimace.

"Tell you what, Matt," he said. "I'll make a deal with you. Drop the 'uncle' or else I'm liable to forget and call you Winky. Sound fair enough?"

"Fair enough—Mitch."

"And I think Beth would like it, too, if you skipped the 'aunt,'" he added. He tossed a wink my way and headed toward the parking lot behind the newspaper building and I went inside and just happened to see Shannon behind the counter.

"You've been neglecting me," she said.

"I know—your old man's a slave driver."

"He hasn't made you work any evenings yet, has he?"

"No, but I've been busy getting unpacked and settled in that room. Now I'm about as settled as I'll ever be and already I've seen more of those four walls than I can stand."

"Think you're ready to take in the sights of our magnificent city?"

"You a good tour guide?"

"The best," she said. "I've lived here all my life and I know every square inch of this town. And with you on the paper, you should have an idea of what's where. I'll pick you up at the hotel at seven."

I pointed a finger at her, like a warning. "Just one thing," I said. "No snipe hunts or anything like that. I'm still pulling cactus spines out of me. Promise?"

Frowning, she bit her lip. "Well, that'll take some of the fun out of it, but okay—I promise. See you at seven."

5

AT TEN MINUTES to seven I looked into the mirror above the wash basin in my room and wasn't very excited about what I saw. I never am. The trouble was, the face in the mirror didn't look like Robert Redford's. Not that it was an awfully bad-looking face, as seventeen-year-old faces go. I don't mean to sound braggy or stuck-up or anything like that; I'm just being objective. I might not be Robert Redford, but at the same time, I'm not Woody Allen, either. On a scale of Robert Redford to Woody Allen, I'm maybe a Dustin Hoffman.

As I said, I'm just a little under six feet tall, and I'm not what you would call beefy, except for my face, which has a lot of cheek. Allison calls it my baby fat. Kid sisters are always saying things like that. My skin is very fair and it burns easily, and in just those few days in Arizona, I had already managed to pick up a lot of color. It almost looked like I was wearing blush. My nose isn't particularly big, but then again, it isn't a little button thing, either. I think I have my father's nose, except that his goes off to one side where it was broken when he played high

school football. I never played high school football, so my
nose is straight. My eyes are deep brown—black,
almost—and my hair is brown, too, and awfully stub-
born. In fact that evening my hair was giving me even
more trouble than usual. I had shampooed and in that
dry Arizona climate my hair was as full of electricity as a
power plant. With the energy crisis I wished they could
have harnessed it. I'll bet Robert Redford never has that
kind of trouble with his hair.

Probably the thing that bothers me most about my
face—besides the fact that it isn't *his*—is that it looks so
young. It worried me that nobody would take a reporter
seriously if he looked like a kid. I was sure that before
the summer was over I'd walk up to some important
news source in Crandall and say, "Hi, I'm Matt Althaus
from the *Chronicle*," and the important news source
would look at me and ask me how many papers I carry on
my route, or can't I try to toss the paper onto the porch,
especially on rainy days. I frowned into the mirror but it
didn't make me look any older, and then I pursed my lips
tight and that didn't help, either. Maybe I should grow a
moustache, I thought, but I knew the summer wouldn't
be long enough for that. If I started growing one now,
maybe somebody might notice it by a year from next
Christmas.

When I was done making faces at myself in the mirror
I went downstairs and waited on the wide front porch of
the hotel. The place had been built about fifty years
before, somebody had told me, and it looked it. It was
close to the old railroad station that had been torn down
several years ago after the main line of the railroad had

been rerouted around Crandall. Mostly old retired men lived in the hotel and I was at least thirty years younger than anybody else I ever saw around there. Off the lobby, where most of the men sat and talked, was a dining room that served pretty good food. It was cheap, too, so I ate most of my meals there. An old cowboy cornered me on the porch and started telling me his life story and we were up to his sixth year when Shan drove up in the Chevy wagon. I told the guy I'd see him later, but I hoped I wouldn't.

There were still a couple of hours of daylight left and Shannon made the most of them. We must have put on sixty miles that night, a lot of them just cruising around town. She was wearing shorts and a halter top and I kept looking at her instead of the sights she was pointing out as she drove. She gave me the whole history of the town. Or towns, rather, because there were two of them.

Crandall had been established in the late 1880s as a headquarters town for a big mining company. They built a smelter there to process copper ore, because although Crandall itself wasn't a mining town, the company had some large copper mines in the area, and Crandall was located fairly close to all those mines.

Of course Crandall was built on the U.S. side of the Mexican border, and its twin city, just beyond the chain-link fence, was a place called La Pizca.

"La Pizca—what does it mean?" I asked one time when Shannon paused for a breath. "The *Pizca* part. *La*, I already know." I laughed. She didn't.

"Pizca means 'speck,' or a 'bit,' or a 'pinch,' like a pinch of salt. When Crandall was built, the Mexican town already was here, only La Pizca was exactly that—just a *speck* of a town."

La Pizca, I said to myself. The Speck. La Pizca, The Bit. Pizca, Pinch. When I got back to my room I'd write it down so I'd remember. I was determined to learn at least ten words every day—more, if I could—to build my Spanish vocabulary. Besides that I'd try to pick up as many Spanish idioms and expressions as I could.

Anyway, Shannon said the two communities had grown up together and now Crandall had a population of about 12,000 and La Pizca had almost 20,000 people living in it.

Downtown Crandall was located almost a mile from the international border. As we drove from downtown toward Mexico, the buildings were older and shabbier, and the businesses had gaudy signs, mostly in Spanish, and the shop fronts were painted in bright colors. Mostly poorer Mexican-American families lived in that area close to the border. The town's nicer residential district was north of downtown. There were a lot of fine old homes close to downtown, including one whole block of them, where mining company executives lived. Everybody called it "the Row." The newest homes in town were those farthest north from downtown. Crandall had been growing slowly but steadily since World War II, and most of the newcomers lived in the large subdivisions north of the downtown area, as did many of the younger Mexican-American families. There was a shopping center out north, which had been built in the last few years because of all the new housing out in that area.

Many Crandall residents worked for the company, Shan told me, either at the central office or the smelter

or at the company store on Copper Avenue, where most
of the company employees and just about everybody else
traded. Some of the local people commuted to the mines
in other towns. Although it was hardly what you would
think of as another Sun City, a surprising number of
retired people lived in Crandall, too.

Besides the mining and smelting, Crandall was also a
center for all the ranching and farming activity in the
area. Cattle was very big in Papago County, she told me,
and up in the northern part of the county there were
some large vegetable farming communities, where lettuce was king. She said that the town was a trucking
center, too, because a lot of the produce grown on the
farms down in Mexico came through the border crossing
at Crandall-La Pizca, and was trucked on to various
parts of the United States.

We had been driving around for barely an hour and
already I knew more about Crandall and La Pizca than I
knew about my own home town. Shannon was a good
guide.

"Has Daddy told you about our ranch?" she asked me.
I told her he hadn't and she was surprised. "Then you
must be the only person in southern Arizona who hasn't
heard all about it—I'll show you."

We drove northwest on the Tucson Highway for about
ten minutes, and then Shannon turned due north at a
junction, onto a smaller state highway.

"Straight ahead up this road, about thirty miles, is
Corinth, the county seat," she told me. "You probably
won't be going up there too often because the *Chronicle*
has a part-time correspondent who lives there and
covers the Papago County Court House for Daddy. You

won't be missing anything though, because Corinth's a pretty grim place. They closed down the mine there a few years ago and laid off just about everybody, so it's the next thing to a ghost town."

For what was probably about fifteen miles we followed the highway, then Shan turned off on a dirt road and drove another mile, stopping at a wide, ranch gate. I got out of the car and opened it and she drove through. She waited there while I closed the gate and got back into the car.

There were signs all around that said, "Posted—No Hunting," and "No Trespassing," and "Private."

"Friendly people, these Garritys," I teased.

Shannon laughed. "We do sound pretty nasty, don't we? But we have such a problem with hunters and picnickers and just plain busybodies, that Daddy finally had to put up all those signs. People would walk off with the place if they had half a chance."

As we drove along the rutted road, Shan warned me not to expect too much, or I'd be disappointed. She was right. She pulled up and parked in front of a small cluster of buildings.

"Daddy just lives for this place," Shannon said. "In a year or two he wants to build a home out here, and eventually leave the newspaper business and spend all his time here."

She pointed out the buildings. There was an old adobe bunkhouse, where Larry lived. Larry, she said, was the ranch's only cowboy who also served as caretaker and watchman for the place. Not far from the bunkhouse was the corral, and next to the corral was a tack shed, where they kept the saddles and bridles and other horse gear.

"But I don't see any horses," I told her, "or cows, for that matter."

"For a city slicker you're very observant. We only have five or six horses right now, and I suppose they're out grazing, and it just so happens that we don't have any cattle yet."

Some ranch, I thought. Six horses, all off hiding, and zero head of cattle.

The only other building on the place was the biggest and fanciest and looked like the newest, too. It was a barn, with a wide door that was closed and padlocked, and it couldn't have been more than a few years old.

"I think if I were that Larry guy I'd move out of that beat-up old bunkhouse and into the barn," I told Shan.

"Oh, I know—it's beautiful. Daddy had it built last summer. We store baled hay and I don't know what else in there. I hardly ever get inside of it, so I don't know for sure. Mom always teases him about its being nicer and more expensive than our house in town."

I looked around. "This place looks deserted," I said to Shan and she nodded.

"Larry must be in town—his pickup's gone. Otherwise I'd introduce you. Not that you're missing anything, believe me. Larry's not much more than thirty or so, but he's like an old hermit. He sometimes acts hateful for no good reason, but Daddy says he does a good job for him out here, so he keeps him on."

"Sounds like Larry and Trevor Brannigan would make a great pair," I said.

"Oh, Bran? He's a pussycat. I just love him! He and

Larry—they're altogether different. Bran tries to let people think he's a gruff old newspaperman, but Larry—he's just plain mean. He's not what you'd call one of my favorite people."

It was beginning to get dark, so we started back toward Crandall. "Have you ever been in Mexico?" Shan asked as we neared town.

I said I'd never been out of the United States and she told me to prepare myself to become an international traveler.

We drove through town and followed Copper Avenue until it jogged off to the right, then drove onto the access road that leads to the crossing gate. We drove right past the U. S. check station and a man in uniform—I later learned that both customs and immigration people do duty at the gate—waved a greeting to us as we passed. Not many yards later we came to the Mexican entry post, where a middle-aged man in a khaki uniform sat on a high stool, his back resting against a pole.

Shan stopped the car beside him and he leaned over, looked inside, then smiled and nodded slightly, signaling to drive on.

"Welcome to Old Mexico!" she said as she stepped down on the gas pedal. Somehow it wasn't quite what I had expected. I had thought I would feel lots different, somehow, being in another country. But I didn't. I felt pretty much the same as I usually do.

In the blocks closest to the border-crossing station there were a lot of liquor stores, curio shops, banks, offices and bars, or *cantinas*. Even though it was almost nine o'clock, a lot of the little shops were still open, and all of the *cantinas* seemed to be.

People stood in groups along the sidewalk, or were seated on the steps, talking, laughing and watching the cars pass. When we pulled up at a traffic light, a small boy, barefoot and carrying a counter-display box of chewing gum, ran up to the car and held the box through Shannon's open window.

"Chewing gum, senorita?" he asked.

"Sure," Shan said, and she reached into the coin purse of her wallet and fished out a quarter. She dropped it into the box and took a tiny packet of chewing gum.

The traffic light turned green and Shan pulled away slowly. *"Gracias,"* the boy called after us.

"It isn't sugarless," she said, handing me the gum to unwrap, "but I don't imagine a little bit will hurt our teeth."

The town square, or *plaza*, was about two blocks from the border, and a lot of people were strolling or sitting on benches, enjoying the coolness of the evening. On one side of the *plaza* was a big, old-looking Catholic church, made of gray stone. The three other sides of the plaza were lined with more tiny shops and offices and some restaurants and more *cantinas*. It was quiet and peaceful and from someplace in the distance came the sound of music. Maybe it came from one of the bars.

As we drove through the streets of La Pizca we came, all at once, to an area of large, expensive homes. Mansions, you'd have to call them. I didn't count them, but there seemed to be maybe two dozen of the big houses, and all of them had high, wrought-iron fences or brick walls around them.

"The rich people, the *really* rich people, live in these places," said Shannon, as if an explanation were necessary. You just *had* to be awfully rich to afford homes like that. We passed through areas of houses that were small and very simple, yet were very neat and well-kept. "A lot of the people who own the shops or work in some of the offices live in those places," she said. "Some of them work in the newer factories, too, and are making quite a bit of money."

By far though, most of the houses we saw were run-down shacks or long, low buildings that were made up of little cubbyhole apartments. "You see so many of these little shacks like this," she said. For a minute or two, she drove in silence. "That's what really is so sad down here, Matt," she said. "There are a few really rich people, but most of the others are terribly poor. For a long time there wasn't much of what we call the 'middle class,' and that's what has caused so many of the problems.

"Daddy says it's getting better now—he says the middle class is growing in number—and now that Mexico is going to be developing all that oil, the situation will be even better. Not right away though—it'll still take time."

Shannon talked on as she drove through the streets of La Pizca. "Down in the interior, especially in the rural areas, there are sometimes strikes and demonstrations. Daddy worries that maybe they're going to have another revolution down there over land reform. As it is, a lot of the poorer people don't have work and those who do, don't get paid very much money, and that's one of the main reasons a lot of them try to sneak into the United States to look for jobs."

"Can they get jobs up in the U. S.?" I asked.

"Most of them manage to, I hear. The American employers know they can hire illegal aliens for less money than U. S. workers, so they take advantage of them. At least that's what Daddy tells me. So they come up here and get jobs and save a few dollars and send what they can to their families down in Mexico."

I was enjoying being with Shannon and it was fascinating seeing the people and buildings and knowing I was in a different country, but I was getting tired. I yawned. It was almost full dark. I looked at my watch.

"I hope it's the hour," said Shan, pretending to sound hurt.

"No," I said, "it's the company. Did anyone ever tell you you're boring?"

"Why, Winky! How can you—"

But that was as far as she got. A dog—hardly more than a puppy—ran out in front of us. Shannon braked, swerving to miss the pup. Both of us braced ourselves and I sucked in a deep breath and shut my eyes and waited. Then we hit with a tremendous jolt.

6

FOR HALF A minute we sat in the car, too stunned to move. Finally I was able to get my tongue working.

"You okay?" I asked Shannon.

"I guess," she answered, leaning forward and turning off the ignition and lights. "Least I will be, once my heart stops pounding. Are you—"

"Don't worry, I'm okay, too. Shook-up, but okay."

"That dog—it just came out of nowhere," said Shannon, making it sound like an apology.

"I know. I didn't even see it until after you swerved. Don't worry, Shan, it wasn't your fault. You did a fantastic job of missing it."

"Well, we missed the dog, but we hit something," she said. "I didn't see anything, but it happened so fast. Now I'm almost afraid to look."

"Got a flashlight?"

"Glove compartment," she said. "If it works."

It worked. Both of us were out of the car in a second and in two seconds I had spotted the problem.

"Over here," I called, shining the flashlight's beam on the front right tire. It was flat, and behind the wheel was a huge rock. The wheel must've hit that rock, blown the tire and jolted right over it.

"Look there," I said as Shan came around the front of the car. I jiggled the beam for emphasis. She whistled, then laughed.

"This is funny?" I asked.

"I'm sorry," she said, gasping for breath, "but it just tickles me. I was thinking, 'how terrible,' when all of a sudden I thought of that old line about the tire just being flat on the bottom."

"Ha-ha," I said, sarcastically as I could. "How are you at changing tires? I've never changed one in my life."

Shannon quit laughing. "Me neither. That's something we never learned in driver's ed."

I looked around. There wasn't a gas station in sight. In fact, there wasn't much of anything in sight. We must've been near the very edge of town because there were only a few small houses nearby. Only one or two of them had lights showing through the windows. Half a block away there was a very dim street light, but that sure didn't help us where we were.

It was creepy, being in a foreign country and then having this happen. I was worried, and I guess even a little bit afraid, but I didn't say a thing about that to Shannon. I was sure she wasn't afraid, because she practically lives in Mexico and knew what to expect. I didn't let on that I was scared.

"I guess about the only thing we can do is to go ahead and change the tire," I said. "*Try* to change it, at least." I knew we'd never learn how to do it just standing there, so I took Shan's keys from the ignition switch, unlocked the rear door of the wagon and then opened the compartment that held the spare and jack and everything.

"You're acting like a real pro," Shan said. "So far it looks like you change flat tires for a living."

"Shut up and hold this flashlight while I get the spare out, will you?"

Shan held the light steady while I undid the watchamacallit that kept the spare in place, and then lifted it out of the well. We were in luck—it was inflated. I rolled the wheel up to the front of the car, then went back for the jack and lug wrench.

When it comes to mechanical stuff, I'm a real bust. I've got two left hands with five thumbs on each. Without any help I did manage to pry the hubcap off, even though I nicked my knuckles, but good. Then I tried to get the bumper jack set in place.

"Before you do that you're supposed to make sure the car is in 'park' and the brake is pulled," said Shannon. I dropped the jack handle and, grumbling, walked around the wagon to set the brake. The car already was in "park." Then I got back to the bumper jack. No matter what I did, I couldn't make it work. The hook-part wouldn't ride up the shaft, if shaft is what you call it. The thing just wouldn't catch.

"Winky, I hate to say this, but before you start jacking the car I think you're supposed to loosen those nut things. I remember watching my Dad change a tire," said Shan.

I quit pumping and counted to ten under my breath. "Who's doing this," I said to her, "me or your father?"

And then without even waiting for her answer, I went back to pumping the jack, for all the good it did. The second I said that I knew I shouldn't have. I quit pumping and looked at Shannon. "I'm sorry," I said to her. She shined the flashlight beam from the jack into my face and I raised my hand to shield my eyes and let out a breath through my teeth.

"Okay," she said quietly. "Apology accepted." Then she shined the beam back on the jack and I took the hint and tried pumping again. The thing just wouldn't catch, the way I think they're supposed to. I took the flashlight from Shannon's hand and aimed it under the hook part that's supposed to slide under the edge of the bumper and raise it, notch by notch. I figured there must be some kind of catch under there that you set to go up or down. I found something that might've been it, and I was working at it, trying to loosen it, when suddenly I saw a movement off to one side, in the shadows.

At once I jumped to my feet, flashlight in one hand, the jack handle in the other. My hands were trembling and I couldn't keep them still.

"Who's there?" I called out, and I shined the light in the direction of the movement. It was a man. He froze, hands about six inches from his hips, like he was a two-gun movie cowboy waiting to draw. The flashlight beam jiggled on him, and for the life of me I couldn't steady it. I hefted the jack handle and stepped out so I'd be between that guy and Shannon.

"Who are you?" I called to him. "What do you want?"

He answered me in Spanish and I couldn't catch a word of it. I raised the jack handle a few inches and held it as though I meant business. The guy took a step backward. He lifted his hands, fingers apart and palms toward me, and he spoke some more in fast Spanish.

"He says to put that iron down," Shannon said. "He doesn't want to hurt us or anything—just help. He says it looked as though we *needed* help." I think Shannon laughed just then, but I'm not sure of it.

Slowly he stepped from the shadows and moved toward us. I kept the flashlight shining in his face. Up close he looked young, maybe just a little older than me, and he didn't look at all mean. The guy was smiling. I breathed easier, but I wasn't taking any chances. I kept a good hold on the tire iron.

Shannon said something to him in Spanish and he answered her.

"His name is Vicente," she told me.

"Does he know how to change a tire?" I asked her. She spoke in fast Spanish—even faster than Mrs. Orth, my old Spanish teacher—and Vicente nodded.

He stepped closer. Shannon rattled off some more Spanish and I heard her say "Matt" and "Vicente." She was introducing us to each other. Smiling even bigger, Vicente reached out his hand to shake. "*Buenos dias,*" I said to him, hoping my pronunciation was okay. We shook. "Good evening," he said. "How do you do?" Vicente made a little bow as he said that.

"You speak English?" I asked.

He shrugged and said, "I are learning." Then Vicente frowned. "Is that how you say—'I are learning'?"

"*Am*, Vicente," said Shan, sounding like a school

teacher. "I *am* learning." He repeated it after her and she nodded.

"Now we fix," he said, taking the tire iron from my hand.

"Is he going to change a tire with those good clothes on?" I asked Shannon. "They look brand new. He'll get them all dirty." Not that the clothes were fancy, or anything. Just a pair of brand-new khaki pants and a white, short-sleeved sport shirt that still had the store folds in it. Shannon spoke to Vicente and he answered her, shaking his head.

"No matter," he said. "I are careful." And then he caught himself. Grinning, he hiked his eyebrows and raised an index finger in the air. "I *am* careful," he said.

Then Vicente was squatting down beside the tire, loosening the lugs. Shannon looked at me, a funny smile on her face. I felt about three inches high. But she didn't say, "I told you so," or anything like that. I moved closer and held the flashlight so that it would do the most good for Vicente. When he had the lugs loosened he went up front, fiddled with the jack for a few seconds, made certain the base was on solid ground and got it all set.

Then Vicente picked up the rock we had bumped over—the one that blew the tire—and carried it behind the left rear wheel and wedged it there to keep the car from rolling back, off the jack. He didn't waste a motion. It was a cinch that Vicente had changed a tire more than just a time or two. In no time he had the car jacked up, the flat tire off, the spare on, the jack pumped down again, the lugs tightened, the hubcap back on the wheel, the flat in the tire compartment and the parts of the jack tucked in there with it.

A couple of times while he was doing all that I tried to help him but he just shook his head and said something I couldn't understand and waved me aside. So I just stood there with Shannon, feeling like a helpless dummy, except that I did a pretty good job of holding the flashlight.

By the time he was finished he had worked up a real sweat, and he was just dripping. He almost looked as though he had run through a lawn sprinkler with those nice new clothes of his. He brushed off his hands then and leaned over to brush at his pants, where he'd been kneeling in the dirt, and I saw a big grease spot on the left knee of his khaki pants. I felt awful. So did Shannon.

"Oh, look at you," she said, and she bent over and wiped at the grease spot with her fingertips. Vicente stepped back quickly, like he was embarrassed by the fuss, and said, "No, no, no—is nothing."

"Oh, but it *is* something," she said. "Your pants— they're ruined."

"I wash them okay," he said, and that was that.

Down the block, under the street light, there was an old man pushing a cart. Shannon spied him, too. "Snow cones!" she said, almost squealing. "Let's get one!" She grabbed each of us by a hand and dragged us down the street. We all laughed and Vicente and I started doing those high, exaggerated skips you sometimes do when you're acting silly. Shannon laughed so hard she couldn't keep up and she stumbled and almost fell, except that we caught her. At first when we skipped Vicente seemed surprised and sort of held back, but then he laughed, too, and skipped even higher than I did. When she was able to quit laughing, Shan ordered for us all. I acted like a big sport and paid. The old man dipped deep into the cart and scooped out crushed ice and packed it in paper cones. He poured red syrup over the ice from one of several bottles on the cart. Talk about slurpy! Walking back to the car I was almost bent over in half trying to keep that sweet, sticky red stuff from dribbling all over me. It tasted good, though. We finished our snow cones and the three of us climbed up onto the front of the car and we sat in the dark, just talking.

Vicente was eighteen, he told us, and he lived near a little town deep down in Mexico. He said the name of the town and I pronounced it after him, but I don't remember now what it was. There were seven kids in his family and he was the oldest. The family lived on a farm, but it was just a small one, and I got the idea that his family was pretty poor.

As we talked I kept trying out Spanish words on Vicente, and he was using English on us. It tickled me that both of us were trying so hard to learn the other's language. But he was way ahead of me. Even though it was slow going for him at times, Vicente was able to really communicate in English, while I was still messing around with "The book is on the table" and "My pen is green" kind of Spanish. I knew I would have to work harder at it. My vocabulary wasn't too bad, but I had a lot of trouble with verb tenses.

Shannon asked Vicente if he was on a vacation and when he didn't answer right away she asked him again, but in Spanish. He still didn't answer right away, but finally he said he had come to La Pizca to live with his uncle. Maybe we could get together again some time, I thought. I'd like that.

"Are you going to be here long?" I asked him.

"*¿Quien sabe?*" he said at last.

It seemed spooky, for some reason. For maybe a half minute he didn't answer, and when he did, there was a funny tone in his voice.

And then right away he started talking about something else, as if he didn't want to talk about what he was doing up there on the border, so far from his home. Then his uneasiness was gone and it was as if we three were old friends. I don't know how long we talked. It seemed like hours, but maybe it was only a half hour or so.

Vicente slid to the ground then and said it was time for him to leave.

"Hey," I said, getting off the fender then, too. "Thanks again for helping us. *Muchas gracias.*"

"Boy, you have a real way with words," Shannon teased. I ignored her, because just then I happened to realize we hadn't even paid Vicente for changing the tire for us and getting his new pants ruined with the grease spot. I opened the car door to turn on the dome light inside, so we'd be able to see.

Turning toward the light, I opened my wallet. It was pretty thin. I had a five and three ones. I decided to pay Vicente five dollars, figuring it was worth every penny of it. We'd have still been struggling with that tire if he hadn't come along. I took out the five dollar bill, folded it in half and handed it to him.

"For you, Vicente," I said. "For helping us."

"No, no," he said, smiling.

"But you earned it—and your pants. They're ruined." In the dim light from the car he studied the grease spot and made a sucking noise with his mouth.

"No," he said, "I do it for my new friends." He had problems with verb tenses, too.

Vicente looked down at that five dollar bill in my hand and for a second I thought he was going to take it, but then he shook his head once more and stood straighter. Pushing my hand away he said firmly, "No." I put the money in my pocket. I realized it would hurt his feelings if I tried to make him take it.

"I hope we see you again," I said. Shannon said she hoped so, too. And then we shook hands.

Smiling, Vicente looked at us and said, "My new friends."

"*Amigo nuevo*," I said, and we all laughed and then he made the "OK" sign with one hand, turned and disappeared into the darkness.

For a minute or two Shannon and I stood there, neither of us speaking.

"Nice guy," I said.

"I liked him," Shannon agreed.

"I hope we get to see him again." When Shannon didn't say anything more I looked at my watch. "It's late," I said. "We'd better head for home."

"Not until you buy me a Coke. I've talked my throat dry, and that snow cone was so sweet, it made me even thirstier."

"Okay," I agreed. "A soda but nothing more. Not until payday, at least."

I held the door while Shannon got into the car, then walked around to the passenger side. For a second I looked off in the direction Vicente had gone. I hoped I'd get to see him again. I really liked him.

7

AT THE BORDER the Mexican official waved us through without even bothering to look into our car, but as we approached the U. S. side, the customs man signalled us to a halt.

" 'Evening, Miss Garrity—how's the family?" he asked.

"Everybody's fine, Mr. Blakely. All of us keeping busy." He nodded, then leaned down to look into the car. "Hello, son," he said. "You're new here?"

"Yes, sir. I'm spending the summer working on the *Chronicle*. Mitch Garrity's sort of my uncle." The man nodded once more.

"Where were you born, please?" He surprised me. He had seemed like a family friend, but I guess he had his job to do.

"In Kansas."

"And did either of you buy anything in Mexico?"

Shannon told him no, that all we'd had was a snow cone. He smiled and nodded again, then waved us on. "Have a good evening, hear?" he said as we pulled away.

"There was nothing to it," I said to Shannon. "They didn't even search us, or anything."

"Mr. Blakely's known me 'most all my life, and besides, I think he and the others can pretty well tell when someone is trying to pull something. They're really sharp. Why, I've seen them tear a VW bus apart, just because the driver seemed a little too friendly or eager to give information, and sure enough, they turned up enough heroin in that bus to give half of Los Angeles a real high. Don't ever try to fool those customs or immigration people, Matt. It doesn't pay."

We stopped at a place on Copper Avenue—the Sugar Bowl, it was called—for the Coke. It was a popular hangout among the high school kids, Shan told me, although there were just a few booths filled when we arrived. I didn't see any of my snipe-hunting buddies, but Shannon introduced me to some friends as we paraded through the place and settled in a back booth.

"The Bowl is dead tonight," she said, almost like an apology. "Tuesdays are always this way. Besides, it's late."

"Is it usually busier?"

"Usually," she said. "It's one of the few places in town where they don't shoo the kids out after five minutes. You can nurse one soda pop all night here and they don't get mad."

A girl took our order and brought the sodas and then we were alone. At least as alone as you can be in a place like the Sugar Bowl, with the juke box turned way up and people laughing and talking loud. I unwrapped my straw and poked it into the glass, took a deep drink and looked up. Shannon was staring at me.

"Why so serious?" I asked.

"Thinking."

"About what?"

"I'm thinking I'm glad you came here this summer. I mean, I like my friends and all, but I've been with most of them since I was real little. You? You're somebody different, Matt, somebody from the outside, somebody I haven't seen every day of my life since I was in kindergarten."

"I don't know what you mean," I said.

"It's not like you, growing up in a big city where there are places to go and things to do all the time. Here, it's the same thing and the same people, day after day. I was really dreading the summer, Matt, even after Daddy told me you were going to be here. I didn't remember you at all, not really. I'm sorry, but I didn't. I thought, oh God, what if he turns out to be a creep?

"I didn't think I would be able to stand it until September, when school starts again, but now I've changed my mind. Seeing you and getting to know you again after all these years—I don't care if September never comes."

I didn't know how to answer her. I mean, no girl had ever talked to me that way before and it took me by surprise. So I just smiled at her. I tried to make it a crooked smile with sort of a wistful look in it, but then I got to worrying that maybe if I looked too wistful it might make me look like I was nauseated and about to throw up, so I straightened the smile and reached out across the table and put my hand over hers. I had to say something, but I didn't know what.

"You might not know this, Shan, but I used to hate you. I mean, when we were together that time when we were kids you were really awful. You know, a big pest. I even had to think twice before I accepted your dad's offer for me to come out here this summer because I was afraid you'd be just as much a pest as before. Worse, maybe."

She smiled. I never noticed before how white and straight her teeth were. She could have been an airline stewardess.

"Are you glad you decided to come down here?" Shan asked.

"Yeah," I said, nodding slowly. "I'm glad. Real glad."

She gave my hand a squeeze and it surprised me so much that I jerked the hand and knocked the Coke into my lap, and I'd had only one swallow.

8

IT TOOK ME almost a week to get it all straight, and
even then I had some questions in my mind.

Within the boundaries of the city of Crandall, the city
police department has jurisdiction. Outside Crandall, in
the rural areas, the Papago County sheriff's office was
responsible for keeping the peace. The main sheriff's
office was at the county seat, up in Corinth, but a couple
of deputies lived in Crandall and covered the southeast-
ern part of the county.

The highway patrolmen were state officers, part of the
Arizona Department of Public Safety, and it was their
job to patrol, give traffic citations and investigate
accidents on federal and state highways. There were
three DPS highway patrolmen assigned to the Crandall
sector. There were a couple of other state public safety
men in the area, but they worked mostly on narcotics
traffic and they weren't what you would call chummy, so
I never really got to know them.

As if that weren't enough, there were a bunch of
federal immigration and customs agents, some in uniform, some in street clothes, some working undercover,

as well as a large border patrol unit. Most of them worked out of the federal building down near the border crossing.

All this was thrown at me that first day Mitch took me on the rounds with him. On top of that, there were the city and county government officials. I met the mayor, who is a florist, a couple of city councilmen, the city clerk—a sweet old man who wore a green eyeshade and sleeve garters—and the police chief, the fire chief, the city magistrate, and the county justice of the peace.

But what really got complicated was when we went across the line—that's what the locals call crossing the border—to La Pizca. Over there, I discovered, almost everybody was an official of some sort, and Mitch seemed to know all of them. He rolled off Spanish with them like he'd been speaking it all his life. Most of the officials in La Pizca spoke English, I learned, but Mitch enjoyed using his Spanish and told me that the Mexican people had more confidence in a gringo who could speak their language, and were apt to provide more information to a newsman who did. I was relieved when Mitch told me not to worry about contacts over there, because he would keep tabs on matters across the line unless something should come up while he was away from the office or out of town.

It was especially important for me to get to know Crandall Fire Chief Manny Garcia and Police Chief Ray Blueford, Mitch told me, but one man who knew a lot about what was happening in Crandall was Police Captain Joe Moreno. He'd be an important police source. Every morning on my way to the office I would have to stop at the police department and read over the reports from the night before, make notes on everything that looked like news, then go to the *Chronicle* office and get those stories written first thing.

Mitch and I went through some of the police reports together one day and he showed me what was news and what wasn't. Barking dog complaints weren't news, but traffic accidents were—even if they were nothing more than fender benders. A family fight wasn't news unless someone was badly hurt or if it involved some unusual circumstances, but thefts, burglaries, vandalism, robberies or anything of that sort were news. "You'll soon get to where you know what's worth writing and what isn't," Mitch told me. "It'll become second nature to you."

We had lunch together at the Crandall House, which was the fanciest hotel in town. All the service clubs held their luncheon or dinner meetings there, and any time a convention was held in town, it was always at the Crandall House. It was an old hotel, just like the Railroad Hotel where I lived, but there the similarity ended. It was very elegant. The Railroad, as I already mentioned, was a hole.

The lobby of the Crandall House had a high ceiling and marble pillars and nice oil paintings on the walls and good furniture that matched. It was fancy and it seemed out of place in Crandall.

Over lunch we talked mostly about the paper, and Mitch provided me with more information about the operation. The daily circulation was about 3,500, he said, and about 2,500 of the newspapers stayed in Crandall—

home deliveries, mostly—and the others went up to Corinth and several other little communities north of us in Papago County.

"How do you get the papers up there?" I asked.

"Fellow named Jess Perry trucks them for us," said Mitch. "Jess has a contract with us to make the run every day. He has a little moving and hauling outfit here and the steady job with us keeps him afloat financially. And it's cheaper for us to pay him to haul the papers than it would be for us to buy a truck and hire a man to drive it."

Perry had a brand new truck, Mitch said. "And it's his pride and joy," he added with a grin. "I think he loves that truck more than he loves his own mother—he's forever polishing it."

I had seen Jess around the building a few times. The paper was supposed to start rolling off the press about 12:30 and Jess always showed up at noon, backing his truck up to the big doors at the rear of the shop. The shop was the one-floor addition to the *Chronicle* building—right behind the business and advertising offices—and that's where our type was set and placed in the big, page-sized forms and then put on the press and printed. Every time I saw Jess he was out there polishing that truck, waiting for the presses to start rolling. I was afraid he'd wear the finish off it.

I told Mitch that one of the printers had told me Jess's name really was Jesus Maria Perez, and Mitch said that was right. "Jess was born down in Sonora—that's the Mexican state just below Arizona—but he doesn't like to think of himself as being a native of Mexico. Fact, he doesn't like anyone else to think of him that way, either.

Won't often speak Spanish and hardly admits that he knows the language. Strange guy, but he does his job. He's dependable and that's why he has the contract."

Mitch asked me then how I was getting along with Bran and I just shrugged. "We talk some," I said, "but we're not what you could call buddies."

"Give it another week or so—all of a sudden one day he'll get used to having you around and he'll loosen up," Mitch said. He smiled. "Not to change the subject, Matt, but you seem to be getting along a little better with Shannie than you are with Bran."

I could feel my cheeks get red. I didn't know what to say. After all, Mitch was my honorary uncle, he was my boss for that summer, and on top of that, he was the father of the girl I was beginning to think very serious thoughts about. So I just said, "Yeah, we're getting to be pretty good friends. She's helped me a lot, learning about the town and all."

"She's a good kid, Matt, if I say so myself. Takes after her mother, of course. Don't let her bulldoze you, though. She has a mind of her own, and she likes to have her way about things. If she gets to bugging you, just stand right up to her."

I told him I would. Then Mitch said he was going to drive down into Mexico and check on some agricultural stories that afternoon, and he sent me back to the office to write some police stories I had picked up earlier. "Bran'll be there—just give him your copy and he'll go over the stories with you." That sounded like a great way to spend an afternoon!

Bran was working on a story when I got back to the office. He typed with only three fingers—the index finger of his left hand and the index and middle fingers of his right—but he typed faster than anyone I've ever known. Even faster than Mrs. Atkins, who was my typing teacher when I was a freshman. Without looking up or missing a letter or even taking the cigar out of his mouth, he grunted his usual greeting to me—"What say, kid?"—and kept right on with his typing. Pussycat, hah!

I spread my notes on the desk, sat down, rolled a piece of copy paper into the typewriter, and in the upper left-hand corner typed my last name, and right below it, the words, "dog bite." Then I sighed. Here I was, wanting to be an investigative reporter and what was I writing about? A newspaper-carrier boy who was bitten by a dog while he was delivering his papers. Big deal. Surely Bernstein and Woodward never had to write about that kind of thing! At the police station I had asked Mitch if the *Chronicle* printed a story every time somebody got bitten by a dog, and he said no. "But two things make this story important," he said, sounding like a teacher. "First of all, he's one of *our* kids—he was bitten while delivering the *Chronicle*. But more important, the dog that bit him ran off. The boy didn't recognize the animal, but he did have a description of it, so if the dog isn't found and checked out for rabies, the kid'll have to have the series of rabies shots, and from what I hear, that's not a lot of fun." When he put it that way, it made sense. Still, it was pretty hard to get enthusiastic about writing a dog-bite story.

So, remembering everything I had ever learned about writing a news story, I went at it. Who, what, when, where, why. The whole business. All the details. All the facts. Short, simple sentences, short paragraphs. I didn't miss a thing. When I finished the story I read it over carefully, checking spellings, age, address, everything. I made some corrections on the paper with a soft-lead pencil, then walked over to Bran's desk with the story. He looked up at me over his steel-rimmed glasses and lifted his eyebrows, which I had learned meant, "Well, what do *you* want?"

"Mitch told me to write a few police stories and have you check them over for me." He grunted.

"Afraid of that," Bran said around his cigar. Taking the story from my hand, he put it on his desk top and read it. Then he looked up at me and shook his head. "Read that second graf aloud," he told me. I did:

"Police said the dog bit young Diaz on his paper route."

"Now tell me, kid," Bran said, "just where on a person's body is his paper route? Between the knee and ankle? Or maybe up around the shoulder?"

I laughed. I couldn't help it. "That's not what I meant to say," I told Bran.

" 'Course it isn't, kid. But it's nothing to laugh about. It's serious; what you write is going to be set in type and printed in the *Chronicle*, and it'll be there forever, in black and white. Try again, but this time think about it and write what you *do* mean."

I retyped the whole story and rewrote that paragraph. When Bran looked it over, he read it aloud:

"The dog bit young Diaz on the left leg, police said. The boy was delivering Wednesday's *Chronicle* at the time he was attacked."

"Now, that's better," he told me, and put the story in the basket with other stories ready to be used. I really felt embarrassed. I went back to my typewriter and looked through my notes. Next I decided to write the story about a man who drove his car into a fire hydrant. I wondered how I'd mess up *that* one. As I put a piece of copy paper into the typewriter, Bran spoke.

"Hey, kid, don't take it hard. Happens to all of us. Don't tell Garrity, but years ago when I was learning the business on the old Chicago *Examiner*, I was covering cops and there was a juicy homicide. I did my story; nobody caught my mistake. And there it was on page one, for all Chicago to read: 'The attractive blonde matron was stabbed in her laundry room.'"

Bran laughed and shook his head. "God, but I was green," he said softly, as much to himself as to me. "They rode me about it—rode me plenty. But I got over it and caught on, kid, and you will, too. You just be careful with your paper route and I'll watch my laundry room."

Both of us laughed then, and soon I went back to my fire-hydrant story, and Bran started his machine-gun typing again, pausing now and then to chuckle to himself.

9

YOU ALWAYS HEAR old people say, "My, how time flies," and I always thought that was pretty dumb, because everybody knows one given hour isn't any shorter or longer than any other. Now I know what they mean though, because those days and weeks in Crandall just seemed to—like they say, *fly!*

Of course I know it was because I was busy and having such a great time that the days seemed to pass so quickly. I worked hard at the *Chronicle* and put in a lot of hours—more than I really needed to—but I was enjoying it and wanted to learn everything I could. But it wasn't just the days that were busy and special.

The evenings were that way, too, and it was Shannon who made them busy and special. We managed to be together, at least for a little while, almost every evening. We'd take a long walk or stop in at the Sugar Bowl and kill an hour or two over Cokes or maybe we'd drive around Crandall or go across the line to La Pizca to shop or eat. Sometimes we stayed home and talked with Mitch and Beth, and if Mitch had to go out, which he did a lot of nights, we'd keep Beth company. Other times we'd listen to records or get together with Maria and Pete and Ernesto and Sandy and Buck and other friends of Shannon's.

Evenings when I wasn't with her, I sometimes rode around in a police car with Tomas Duarte, a young cop who worked the three-to-eleven shift. I had started dropping in at the police station whenever I passed by, or if I didn't have anything else to do. I'd talk with the officers on duty in the station and read through the reports so that I'd know what was going on in town. Usually Tomas was out in the field on patrol, but one evening he happened to be working in the police station, filling in for the desk sergeant, who was sick. That was the night I met him.

When I walked into the station he pushed his chair away from the desk that held the radio console, and walked over to the counter. Smiling, he asked if he could help me. I introduced myself and he smiled even bigger and reached over the counter to shake hands.

"Hey, I heard about you," he said. "I'm Tomas Duarte. It's good to meet you, Matt."

"Yeah," I answered, "it's nice to meet you, Tom."

"Hey," he said sharply, hiking his eyebrows and raising a finger. "To-*mas*, if you please, Matt, not 'Tom.' All my friends call me Tomas, or they don't stay my friends." He laughed.

"To-*mas* then," I said, feeling a little foolish. "I'm sorry."

"Nothing worth being sorry about—it's just a *thing* with me. Tom or Thomas or Tommy are okay for some guys, but not me. My parents named me *Tomas*, and I like that, with the old Spanish spelling and pronunciation. 'Tom' just sounds a little too gringo for me."

Tomas was proud of his heritage, he told me—proud of the Spanish and Indian blood that flowed through his veins. As he said that his chest puffed out and, unless it was my imagination, he seemed to stand taller. Just then I didn't mention it, but I almost laughed to myself when Tom—Tomas—told me that. He felt exactly the opposite of Jesus Perez, who wanted everybody to call him Jess Perry. Jess pretended he wasn't Mexican-American. It was almost as if he was ashamed of it for some reason, while my cop friend was really proud that his roots were in Mexico. Sometimes it's hard to figure out people.

That first evening Tomas and I talked a long time and as I was leaving he invited me to ride around with him some evening. Two nights later Shan was busy so I took him up on his offer. Tomas and I got along real well and after that I rode with him often at night. It gave me a better idea of how policemen work, and besides, it taught me more about Crandall, which helped my reporting.

On Saturdays we worked until noon, when our weekend paper came off the press, and I had Saturday afternoons and all day Sunday to myself. Sometimes on Saturday afternoons I went swimming with Shan at the country club or in somebody's backyard pool, and then had dinner with the Garritys. Sundays were for doing my laundry at the laundromat, writing a letter to my family, straightening my room and always Sunday dinner at Beth and Mitch's house. I didn't have much time to spend being homesick.

On the job I was doing more and more interesting things. One noontime I went to the Crandall House and covered a Lions Club luncheon meeting; the speaker was a state legislator who talked about the water problem in Arizona. That might not sound very exciting, but it was the first speech I ever covered and Mitch said I did a good job. I wrote two-and-a-half pages double-spaced and the *Chronicle* carried almost the whole story as I wrote it on page one, and with very little editing. I didn't get a by-line on that story, but I knew it came closer than any story I had written for the *Chronicle* up to then.

In that same issue, across the top of page one, we ran an Associated Press feature story on the illegal alien situation. It said that the main problem seemed to be that illegal aliens—citizens of other countries, in this case, mostly Mexicans, who had come into the United States illegally—were taking jobs away from American citizens and from legal alien workers.

The story reported that a high government immigration official said in a speech somewhere that the illegal alien situation was "hopelessly out of control." The official said that there were about eight million illegal or undocumented aliens in the country, and that it cost the U. S. taxpayers $13 billion a year in "public services and welfare and several billion dollars a year more in jobs taken from citizens."

I stopped right there and tried to imagine what thirteen billion of *anything* might be. Then I remembered something my freshman algebra teacher had said.

It may have been a little fuzzy in my mind, but I don't think so. He said that if a person started counting numbers—beginning with the number one, of course— and around the clock counted one number each second beginning with the very second of his birth, by the time he reached one billion, he would be more than thirty-one years old. I always remembered that because it seemed so amazing to me. A man would be more than four hundred years old by the time he counted to *thirteen* billion at that rate.

In one recent year almost a million illegal aliens had been apprehended in the United States, the story said. But for every person caught by the border patrol or other immigration officers, two and sometimes three were known to get through undetected. That meant that in that one year alone, somewhere between two and three million illegal aliens had made it safely into this country.

Of course what drew them up across the border was the possibility of finding jobs. "A Mexican who earns the equivalent of $4 a day in his own country can make $16 to $20 in the United States if he can cross the border and avoid the law enforcement officers," the article said.

The more I thought about it, the more I was convinced that those men I had that run-in with on the night of the snipe hunt were illegal aliens. As I sat reading that story, I laughed to myself. Here I was, wanting to be an investigative reporter, and darned if I hadn't run headlong into a big story without even realizing what I had done.

Later that afternoon, after things were quiet in the

office, I asked Mitch what he knew about illegal aliens. He looked surprised. "What makes you ask that, Matt?"

"Our page-one story today," I said. "It made me wonder."

Mitch smiled. "Those figures are really something, aren't they? They get a person to thinking."

I agreed. "I know. It got *me* to thinking and that's why I asked. I'd like to know more about it—the illegal aliens, I mean."

"Let's see what we can come up with," he said, getting out of his swivel chair. It squeaked. Mitch's chair always sounded as though it needed a good oiling. Mitch walked across the newsroom to one of the old green file cabinets, pulled out the bottom drawer and ran his fingertips over the labels on the row of dusty manila envelopes in it. He pulled one envelope from the drawer, and holding it with one hand, gestured toward the open drawer with the other.

"The big city newspapers can afford fancy libraries— 'morgues,' they used to call them—with hundreds of thousands of items in them, filed and cross-filed, and they have huge collections of reference books," Mitch said. He laughed. "The Crandall *Chronicle*? We have one eleven-year-old dictionary, a two-year-old almanac and the bottom drawer of a file cabinet."

Mitch explained that the envelopes in the drawer held clippings of newspaper stories or magazine articles dealing with subjects of particular interest to the *Chronicle*'s circulation area. "We have envelopes for ranching and farming and mining, for the water problem in Arizona, and it just happens we have one with information about illegal aliens," he said, and he handed it over to me. "Go ahead and look through it—you'll probably learn a thing or two. And while you have it out, you'd better clip today's piece and put it in the envelope with the others."

I wrote a few more news stories that afternoon, then tucked the envelope beneath my arm and took it home with me, if you can call the Railroad Hotel "home."

Before going out to dinner I sprawled on my bed and opened the envelope. A lot of the clippings in it were from the *Chronicle*, but most of them were from the bigger papers in Tucson and Phoenix. There were a couple of articles snipped from the news magazines and a long one, "The Flight of the Wetbacks," from the New York *Times Magazine*. I read them all.

I won't pretend that reading them made me any kind of an expert on illegal aliens, but it really taught me a lot. The border between Mexico and the United States is almost two thousand miles long, and it's impossible for the border patrol to be everywhere along that border at one time. So huge numbers of aliens wait until they think the coast is clear and then just sneak into this country by themselves.

Almost everything I read seemed to be sympathetic toward the illegals. You couldn't really blame them for wanting to better their living conditions. Who wouldn't want to make as much in an hour in the U. S. as he had been earning in a whole day in his own country? It's the smugglers, I learned, who are really the bad guys in the whole thing.

They take advantage of the poor Mexican people and

charge them huge amounts of money to get them into this country. Some of them work in organized rings, with contacts down below the border, and they herd large groups of aliens across the line and then transport them north to large cities well above the border, like Los Angeles or Chicago, where the illegals can just sort of melt into the population. The smugglers, or "coyotes," as they are called, charge the aliens as much as $1,000 each. Some people would work for years to save up enough money to pay a smuggler to get them into this country. So smuggling was a big and profitable business.

Of course not all of the illegal or undocumented aliens went to the cities. Some stayed in rural areas and got farm or ranch jobs. Those who did go to the cities usually got unskilled jobs in factories, car washes, or laundries, or as restaurant busboys or dishwashers—the kinds of jobs that were low-paying by U.S. standards and that a lot of American citizens weren't too eager to have unless they were really hard up.

One of the articles said that the people who hire undocumented aliens were almost as bad as the smugglers, because they encouraged the illegals to work for them, knowing they could pay them less than they'd have to pay U.S. citizens to do the same jobs.

As for the aliens themselves, when they were caught by the immigration officers, they were just sent back to Mexico and chances were they'd try to make it across again the next day. Sometimes they were held for a short time and then sent back, but usually they weren't tried and sentenced to jail or anything like that, because they weren't criminals.

Nor were all of the illegal aliens from Mexico. There were some from just about every country in South and Central America, with a lot of them being from El Salvador and Guatemala and Colombia. Mostly though, they were Mexicans.

So it was a tremendous problem and one that wouldn't be solved very easily or very soon. For a while I sat on the bed reading and thinking and trying to figure out how my scrape with illegal aliens—if that's what they really were—fit into the picture. Were those people who I had heard talking that night beyond the hill—and especially my two *amigos*—truly illegal aliens? Or were the two men smugglers? Or were the whole bunch of them just out for a nighttime picnic? Or none of the above? I realized I could scratch the picnic. Those two I tangled with weren't in what you would call a picnic mood, but at the same time they treated me better than they might have. The two of them could have beaten me to a pulp without any trouble at all, and just left me lying there in the desert, but they didn't. Instead they helped me get the cactus stickers out of my arm and side. I happened to glance at my watch as I thought about those two men and just about flew off the bed. I had read and daydreamed right through the dinner hour. By now the hotel coffee shop would be closed and in another fifteen minutes Shannon would be picking me up. Not that we had anything special planned; we hardly ever did. We were just going to spend the evening together.

I raced down the hall to the bathroom set aside for male guests of the hotel and took the world's all-time quickest shower, pulled on a clean pair of Levi's and a sport shirt, and was waiting on the front steps of the hotel—tying the laces of my sneakers—when Shan pulled up.

"What are your big plans for tonight?" she asked as I climbed into the station wagon.

"Food," I said. "Right now that's *numero uno* in the plans department."

"Wow, I'm impressed," she said. " '*Numero uno*'— why you'd think you'd been speaking Spanish all your life. Your accent is very good."

"I guess I'm a natural-born linguist, but don't change the subject—I'm hungry. I got involved and didn't have time to eat in the coffee shop."

"Mexican food?" she asked.

I shook my head. I was developing a taste for Mexican food, but right then it didn't sound very good. "How about pizza?"

"We had pizza for dinner tonight," Shan said.

So we went to the Sugar Bowl. We usually did. I had a burger with fries and a milk shake and Shannon settled for iced tea.

She waited until I had a mouth full of food and then she asked what I was so busy doing that it made me forget about eating.

I made a face at her while I chewed, and after I had swallowed, I told her I'd been reading the *Chronicle*'s files on illegal aliens. "I'll bet *that* was thrilling," she said sarcastically.

"It was," I said, "it really was." I took another bite, chewed, swallowed and then took a mouthful of milk shake. "Shan, did you know that in Los Angeles alone, there are supposed to be more than one million illegal aliens living and working?"

She shook her head and I went on. "One study says that 10 percent of the entire population of Mexico is now in the United States illegally. Think of it—one out of every ten Mexicans."

"That's hard to believe, Matt," she said. The sarcasm was gone from her voice. She frowned thoughtfully. "I mean, all my life, living here on the border, I've been hearing about the illegal aliens—the fence jumpers or the wetbacks as people used to call them—but you know, we'd always think of them as just being one or two people at a time, sneaking across, but it's so different when you get up into the millions. . . ." Shannon let her words just drift away, and her face took on a thoughtful look.

I worked on my hamburger for a bit, then asked her what she was thinking about.

"Those people," she said. "Those poor people down there in Mexico. I know it's really trite—I mean everybody says it—but we don't know how lucky we are. Daddy's traveled all over Mexico and he says there's a lot of poverty down there, but at the same time things are improving with the new oil discoveries and all.

"And Mexico's a lot better off than some of the Central American countries, he says. Still, it's bad enough that you can't blame the people for trying to make better lives for themselves by sneaking across the border and looking for jobs."

"You know, Shan," I said, "I'd really like to see Vicente again and talk with him about what life is like down there. I'll bet he'd tell us the truth about it."

Shan nodded, then reached across the table, poured ketchup on my french fries and began eating them. "You mind?" she asked. I said I didn't. I really did mind though, because I hate ketchup on french fries.

"Go ahead," I said, pushing my plate closer to her. "I've almost had my fill. You finish 'em up." I turned sideways in the booth, with my back against the wall and my legs sticking straight out.

"I don't know if I should tell you this," Shan said between mouthsful of ketchupy french fries, "but Daddy is really pleased with the work you're doing this summer."

"Oh," I said, "I'm glad—I like working on the *Chronicle*, too. I'm really trying to do my best."

"He can tell, I know he can tell." She was silent for a few seconds, then went on. "I think Daddy's always been sorry he didn't have a son of his own—just me. I think, Matt, that he looks on you as being—well, sort of his son. A special, unofficial son. He's proud of you, Matt—very proud."

Hearing Shan say that made me feel good, because that was the way I thought about Mitch. He was sort of a second father to me. He was very special. I didn't know how to answer her, so I just sat staring across the restaurant at the far wall. Finally I changed the subject.

"You know," I said, "I keep thinking about that first night when you took me snipe hunting."

"You're not still angry about that, are you?"

"Oh, no—in fact I don't think I was ever really *angry* about it. That's not what I mean. I'm talking about those guys I wrestled with. I'm positive that was a bunch of illegal aliens down there and that the truck belonged to smugglers, and that I interrupted things at just the right time."

"The *wrong* time, you mean."

"Okay, the wrong time. Anyway, I think I'm going to nose around and see what I can find out. It must be some kind of a smuggling operation. I'd like to do some investigating and maybe write a story exposing an alien smuggling ring, if I can get all the facts.

"Who knows—I might even win a Pulitzer Prize. I'll bet I'd be the youngest person ever to win one."

Shannon smiled, but then her face turned serious.

"Matt—that sounds like it could be dangerous."

"Winning the Pulitzer Prize?"

"Be serious—I don't mean that. I mean poking your nose into that smuggling. The kind of people who must be involved in something like that are probably awfully rough."

I shrugged. "Probably," I agreed. "But I'd be careful, don't worry about that. Besides, chances are I'd never even get into it that deep. I don't have a whole lot to go on."

Shan's smile came back. "You sound like some detective on TV—'much to go on.'"

I wadded up my napkin and flung it at her. She caught it and threw it back. Then we both sat quietly for a while.

"What do you think Daddy'll say?" she asked finally.

"Nothing. At least not unless I do happen to turn up something. I don't plan to tell him or Bran, either, for that matter. And I want you to promise me that you won't tell your Mom or Dad or anyone, okay?"

She looked troubled. "Your folks—they'd be furious, I know, if they thought you were up to something like this."

"That's why we won't tell anyone. It'll just be the two of us. Come on now, do you promise?"

"I guess so, but be careful, hear?" She reached across the table and placed her hand over mine and squeezed it and I dropped my feet to the floor and swung around to face her.

"Okay, it's a deal. I promise to be careful and you promise not to tell Mitch and Beth. It's just between us—our secret." After it came out of my mouth I realized how dumb it sounded—"our secret"—but I didn't say anything about that.

Shan nodded and smiled, but it wasn't much of a smile. She looked troubled.

"If it turns out, though, that you do run into something," she said, "and it looks like you're getting in deeper than you had planned on, promise me you'll get help."

"I promise," I said. But I didn't tell her I had my fingers crossed under the table.

It was my story and I didn't want to share it with anyone.

10

THAT EVENING SHANNON had a surprise for me, such as it was.

All along I had been griping about not having any transportation, and how tough it was to walk all over town getting my stories. "This job," I'd grumbled to Shan, "would be a lot easier, if only I had some wheels."

That was her surprise—wheels. Only they weren't mounted on an auto. After we left the Sugar Bowl that evening we drove out to the Garrity place. Their little second car wasn't in the carport, which meant Mitch and Beth weren't home. We went through the house to the patio, and there, resting against the wall, was my surprise.

It was Shannon's old bicycle, and I really do mean *old*!

"Daddy got it out of the storeroom," she said, "and we cleaned it up and oiled it and everything, and then we took it down to the gas station and pumped up the tires." She sounded awfully proud of herself.

"It's great," I told her, trying to sound enthusiastic, and she looked at me as if she expected me to say more than that, so I did. "It's *really* great, fantastic," I added. I didn't know what else to say.

"It's almost an antique," she told me, although I could tell that just by looking at it. "It was Mom's when she was little—I think it was more in style, then."

It wasn't a ten-speed. It wasn't a three-speed. In fact it was barely a *one*-speed, I later discovered. It had a heavy frame painted an ugly shade of green, and the tires were those big, fat balloon tires that you hardly ever see anymore. The worst thing though, was that it was a girl's bike. She meant well. It's the thought that counts.

I think Shan could see that I wasn't all that thrilled about the bike. "We thought it might make it a little easier for you to get around," she said, sounding almost like she was apologizing. "But you don't have to—"

"Oh, but I *want* to," I said. "Believe me, that bike's going to save me a million steps a day. I'll be able to make my rounds a lot faster with it. It's really great, Shan." What else could I say?

It was still light so we wheeled it out to the front of the house and I invited Shan to go for a ride.

"Not on your life," she said. "At least not until you pedal it around a little bit and get used to it. Maybe then." So I rode up to the corner of the block and then back. They aren't making bikes like that one anymore, fortunately.

"I've mastered it," I said as I pulled up in front of her. "Hop on."

Shannon climbed onto the handlebars and off we went.

Once we got rolling, it wasn't bad. You really have to pump those old bikes though, especially if you're carrying a passenger. We just kept heading up their street and before we knew it we had passed the country club and a half mile after that the pavement ended and the city street became a country road.

I was acting silly and weaving back and forth on the road and Shannon was yelling at me to be careful one minute, then shrieking with laughter the next. Her long, blonde hair was flying up in my face and half the time I couldn't see where we were going.

"This is just like the bicycle scene in *Butch Cassidy and the Sundance Kid*," I said.

"Almost," she said, "except you aren't Paul Newman."

"So maybe you think you're Katharine Ross?" We both laughed. All of a sudden it was hard to steer and the bike started acting up. I let it slow to a stop, then dropped my feet to the ground and held the handlebars steady as I could.

"Quick," I said, "off you go. We've got problems."

"What is it?" she asked, jumping off.

"Flat tire."

"Oh, Winky, I'm sorry."

"It's not your fault—you didn't let the air out."

"Oh, I know, but I should have known better. The bike's been in that hot old storeroom for years. We should've bought new tires, or at least new tubes."

"We can worry about that later," I said. "Right now we'd better get back to your place. Hope you feel like walking." I looked down at her feet. As usual Shan was barefoot. Like most of the kids in southern Arizona, she wore shoes only when she had to. I really had to hand it to her. As pebbly and rough as that road was, she didn't complain once. I asked her if she wanted to wear my shoes, and she laughed.

"I could take three steps inside your shoes and they'd stay in the same place," she said. "I don't mind the rocks, really I don't. I'm used to it."

So we tromped along, slowly while we were on the unpaved road, then faster after we came to the asphalt. I wheeled the bike between us, trying to keep the front, flat tire raised a bit to keep from hurting it any more than it already was. Once we got onto the pavement Shannon came around the bike and walked on the other side of me and slipped her hand under my arm.

It was a nice night for a walk—even an unexpected one. Once the sun had gone down it had begun to cool off, the way it usually does in that desert country, and it was pleasant. We talked the whole way back to the Garritys' house, but not about anything special. I didn't want to mention illegal alien smuggling or anything like that, and I hoped that Shan wouldn't bring up that subject either. I knew she wasn't too keen on the idea of my investigation as it was, and I didn't want to get her thinking about it again. So we talked about school and friends and teachers and about funny things that had happened to us, and we talked about our families and about what we wanted to do when we finished high school and a lot of other things like that.

"How about you, Shan? You've never told me what you want to do."

"You mean what I want to be when I grow up?" she teased.

"I guess that's what I mean."

"Would you believe I don't know?" Shannon said. "I do know I don't want to be a ballerina or an airline stewardess or a nurse or anything else little girls are supposed to want to be."

"That's a pretty negative answer."

"I'm sorry, Winky, but I'm not like you, knowing since you were in diapers what you wanted to be."

"But you must have some idea."

"There are lots of things I'm interested in—you know, like archaeology maybe, and astronomy and things like that—only I want to have a year or two of college before I even think of making a decision."

"Me, I can't imagine going into anything besides journalism," I put in.

"I know, but that's you. Me, I can't imagine *going* into journalism. I mean, I've grown up with it, with Daddy and the *Chronicle* and all. I want to do something different."

"You will," I said, and I meant it. If anybody I knew could be whatever she wanted to be, it was Shannon Garrity.

Walking with her along that dark road, talking and wheeling that dumb bicycle, I realized all of a sudden how much I was going to miss Shan.

"You going to miss me when I'm gone?" I asked her.

"Of course. I imagine I'll just pine away to nothing."

"Be serious."

"I am being serious. I'll just wither away from missing

you. Maybe I'll go into a convent."

"You're not Catholic."

"Do you have to be?"

"I don't know. I just figured you did. I mean, I don't know any *Protestant* girls who ever went into a convent."

"Do you know any Catholic ones who did?" Shan asked.

"I guess not, but I'll bet more Catholic girls go into convents than Protestant ones."

"Maybe I could turn."

I ignored that, then asked, "Will you write to me?"

"I don't know. Do they let you write letters in convents?"

"Come on, I mean it, seriously. Will you write?"

"I'm an awful letter writer. I never know what to say."

"Just write about what you're doing and about school and what you're thinking—things like that."

"Do you really want me to write to you, Matt?"

"I wouldn't have asked if I didn't."

"Okay, then I'll write," Shan said.

"Don't say it that way. I don't want you to write to me just because *I* want you to—I want you to write to me because *you* want to do it." I stopped wheeling the bike and turned to face her, letting the bicycle lean against my back.

"That's awfully confusing, but I think I understand," she said. Shan looked up at me and put her hands on my shoulders and laced her fingers behind my neck.

"Yes," she said softly, "I *will* write to you, Winky. I *want* to write to you."

We kissed and then Shan laughed.

"What's so funny?"

"Us," she said. "I've never been kissed in the middle of the street before."

What she said tickled me and I laughed. "It wasn't *that* funny—what I said," she told me.

"What part of your body is the *middle of the street*?" I asked.

"I don't get what you mean."

"You said I kissed you in the middle of the street—I meant to kiss you on your lips." I laughed some more. She still didn't. So then I told her about the way Bran teased me because I wrote that the dog bit the boy on his paper route, and then I laughed some more, and between laughs I told her about the woman who was stabbed in her laundry room.

Shan still didn't think it was awfully funny. I guess you have to be in the newspaper business to see the humor in it.

"Oh, that's stupid," she said, and she drew back her foot and kicked me. I saw it coming and dodged and she kicked the bicycle right above the sprocket, and howled with pain.

We were still two blocks from her house and she limped all the way. I think she was faking, but just in case she wasn't, I didn't laugh at her at all.

11

IT WAS IN the evening of the day that Bran locked himself in the bathroom and wouldn't come out, that things began to happen. I had read over the illegal alien smuggling file a couple of more times and made some notes from the clippings, which I kept in my room, but I hadn't done anything more than that because I actually didn't know where to start. Besides, I was plenty busy, just doing my routine reporting for the *Chronicle*.

That day Bran was on desk. He and Mitch traded off working desk, which wasn't a whole lot of fun. Working desk was a tough job, because it was the desk man who put the whole paper together each day. He read and edited the copy—what we wrote locally, as well as the news stories that came in over the Associated Press teletype and those that came by mail from the feature services—and then decided which stories we would use and then whether we would use them on page one or on an inside page. He also had to dummy, or lay out, page one, and decide what size headline type would be used on every story, and write all the headlines. What made it especially hard was that the desk man had to work fast and be accurate and make decisions right on the spot as to just how important a given news story might be. Lots of pressure on the desk man.

The other two of us would do the writing, which suited me just fine, because I was more interested in that than I was in writing headlines and editing stories and doing makeup. So on that day Bran was on the desk and Mitch and I were turning out copy like we were machines. I had plenty to keep me busy. There was a story on the summer bowling league that I was working on, and I had five or six police stories to write about minor auto accidents and burglaries and things like that.

Mitch took a story over the phone from the woman up in Corinth who covered county government and the county courts for us, and then he ducked out for a cup of coffee. After that he was going to the city building to sit in on a zoning hearing and right from there he would go to lunch—he was meeting somebody for an interview— so that left just Bran and me in the office for the rest of the morning.

Bran was leaning over his desk making a layout for page one. The deadline was about forty-five minutes away. The page-one copy was spread out on the desk in front of him and he was trying to decide which story would have the banner headline that day. That's when the buzzer rang.

It surprised me because I'd never heard it before. There were three short buzzes, a pause, then three more buzzes.

Bran dropped his pencil and jumped up. His face was almost white.

"Are you sick?" I asked.

"Tell her I'm not here!"

"Tell who?"

"*Her*—you'll see. Tell her I'm out and you don't know where I am or when I'll be back. Tell her I may not *ever* come back."

"But where'll you be?"

"In the bathroom," he said pointing in that direction with his unlit cigar.

"But—"

"Never mind—just get rid of her and let me know when she's gone!"

He turned and hurried across the newsroom and down the hall. There were footsteps coming from the stairs and just as I heard the bathroom door close and the lock snap, a woman reached the top of the steps and said, "Good morning." Actually she sang it more than said it.

"Hi," I said. "Can I help you?"

"Yes, I'm looking for . . . Trevor."

"He's not here right now. He had to leave the newsroom," I said, which was the truth.

"Did Trevor say when he'd be back?"

"No, ma'am," I said. "You're sure I can't help you?" I told her my name and said I was working for the *Chronicle* that summer. She didn't seem impressed.

"I'm Mrs. Fitzhugh," she announced, "and I'm publicity chairman for the Crandall Women's Club."

She appeared to be about fifty and she was a nice-looking woman, for being that old. Her hair was fixed carefully and she wore clothes that were much dressier than what most of the women wore around town. She smelled like a flower shop and carried an umbrella, even though it hadn't rained since my first night in town.

When she told me she was publicity chairman of the women's club she said it as if she expected me to bow or salute or something. Instead, I said, "Oh," with about as much feeling as I could put into it.

"Our summer tea dance is coming up next month—it's *the* social event of the summer—and I wanted to give Trevor the complete story," she said. "He always gives us the *nicest* write-ups."

"Yes, ma'am, but Mr. Brannigan is out of the office and I really don't have any idea when he'll be back. If you'd like to leave your phone number I can have him call you when—"

"Thank you, young man, but that won't be necessary. I'll wait for him." She stepped to the straight-backed chair beside Bran's desk, brushed off the seat with a piece of Kleenex, and sat down. I got back to my bowling-league story and had just about finished it when Harvey, the shop foreman, came up the steps wanting to know where Bran was. I just told him he was out. There wasn't anything else I could say. Harvey said that if we expected to put out a paper that day, they needed the page-one copy and headlines and the dummy. He sounded gruff, but that's just his way. I told him I'd get at it and he stomped down the stairs.

Mrs. Fitzhugh sat taking it all in. "When Mr. Brannigan gets back he's going to be awfully busy," I said to her, hoping she'd take the hint. She didn't.

"That's perfectly all right, young man, I understand. I have plenty of time. I'll just wait." I sighed. I didn't know what to do. She was a real pain, all right. It wasn't hard to see why Bran avoided her, but I was surprised that he would hide in the bathroom when she came around. That seemed to be going awfully far.

In school I had done some makeup on our bi-weekly paper and edited copy and written plenty of headlines, and during the weeks in Crandall I had written a few heads now and then, but I was far from what you would call experienced.

Stepping over to Bran's desk I looked at the copy he had spread over it and just shook my head. I had no idea where to start. For a while I thought about taking all the copy and the dummy forms into Bran in the bathroom, but decided that wouldn't be a very good idea because there just wasn't any room in there to spread out all those papers, and besides, Mrs. Fitzhugh would get suspicious.

There was nothing to do but put together page one myself. Harvey would be stomping up those steps again before long, screaming for copy, so I sat down in Bran's chair and got to work. Anything to keep Harvey happy.

The most important story seemed to be an AP dispatch out of Washington, D. C., about a Congressional hearing on organized crime, so I decided to use it as the lead, or banner story. I edited the story, marked it in on the dummy sheet and then rolled up the story with the headline I had written, put a rubberband around it and dropped it down the chute into the shop. That would keep Harvey happy for a few minutes.

Putting together the rest of the page was just like doing a jigsaw puzzle. I placed stories here and there on the page, and I arranged the two photographs so that they would balance each other and give the page a good appearance. As fast as I'd edit, or copyread, a story and write a headline for it, I'd drop it down the chute. The big old clock in the newsroom showed that I still had two minutes left before deadline when I sent the last story flying down the chute. Then I collapsed in Bran's chair.

"How exciting," said Mrs. Fitzhugh. "I find the newspaper business absolutely fascinating!"

"Yes, ma'am," I agreed, "it sure is." And then I remembered poor Bran, locked up in the bathroom all that time. He'd be furious. I had to think of something.

"Why, I could just sit here all day watching you people work. It's so interesting."

That was all I needed—for her to sit there all day. Then it came to me.

"If you'll excuse me, ma'am, I'd better go down to the shop and check on page one," I said to Mrs. Fitzhugh. "I'll be back in a minute."

I hurried downstairs, through the business office and into the back shop. Harvey had things under control. Well, pretty well under control. "You were a shade off in some of your measuring," he told me. "We had to drop the last few grafs on the school board story to make it fit. Not a bad job though, Matt."

I grinned, soaking up those nice words, and then I thought of Bran. I thanked Harvey and went up front to the business office. Shannon was at the counter taking a classified ad from the man who ran the used-furniture store down near the border.

Excusing myself I broke in and pulled Shan aside. "I'll explain later," I said, "but in two minutes dial the newsroom extension and when I get on the phone, don't pay any attention to what I say, because it won't make any sense. Okay?"

"My mother doesn't like me to call up boys," she said, her face a deadpan. "She says that's pushy."

"Come off it—it's urgent! Just do what I say, okay?"

Shan shook her head. "All my life I've been in a newspaper family and I still don't understand what it's all about. But all right—I'll call you, even if it is a tacky thing for a girl to do."

I took the steps two at a time and stumbled on the top one and would have sprawled across the newsroom floor if I hadn't caught myself. Seated in my own chair I read through my notes on one of the fender-bender stories, twisted a piece of copy paper into the typewriter and began pecking away. By the time I had written the first line and a half, my phone was ringing. I cleared my throat and picked up the telephone.

"*Chronicle* newsroom, Matt Althaus speaking," I said, and then I paused. It was Shan, good old dependable Shan, right on the second.

"Hi, Winky," she said, "guess who this is?" I sucked in a sharp breath, hoping Mrs. Fitzhugh hadn't heard Shan's dumb squealing. I ignored what Shan said.

"Oh, hi," I said nonchalantly into the phone. Shan said something back, but I didn't pay attention to her. I just tossed in an assortment of "ohs," and "uh-huhs," and "hmmmms," and a "good," or two, and then said, "Okay, I'll tell him. Thanks—s'long, Bran."

And then quickly, before Mrs. Fitzhugh could say that she wanted to have a word with Bran, I hung up the phone. "That," I announced to her, "was *Trevor*. He's all involved in a story—you know, sort of a hush-hush thing—and he couldn't even tell me what it was all about. He's afraid he won't get back to the office this afternoon and for all he knows, he might not even get in tomorrow. You know how the newspaper business is," I added.

Mrs. Fitzhugh looked like she was ready to explode, and I made certain I stayed out of her umbrella range. Finally though, she half-smiled and stood. "Yes," she said, as if she had a big ice cube in her mouth, "I know how the newspaper business is."

I walked down the stairs with her and opened the door. As she stepped outside I could hear the presses starting up, so I walked out to the back shop and stood there watching and grabbed one of the first papers off the press. I unfolded it and put it on a shop table and had a good look at page one. *My* page one. It wasn't *too* bad, really, for a beginner. Shan came back to the shop and walked over to where I stood.

"Have a look at that," I said to her, rapping my fingernails on the paper. "I did page one today."

"Well, good for you," she said, and she came closer and elbowed me in the ribs. She looked at the paper about two seconds, then looked at me. "But what I want to know about is that dumb phone call. I've known some weird people in my life, but—"

Suddenly I remembered Bran. Bran! Still locked up in that hot little bathroom! Without saying a word to Shannon I raced through the shop, into the business office and took the stairs three at a time. He'd be furious with me, I knew, because he'd been locked up in there for the better part of two hours.

12

"BRAN," I CALLED through the door, and then I rapped on it. "Bran? Are you in there?"

"Who is it?" came a hushed voice from inside.

"Me, Matt."

"Is she gone?"

"She's gone."

"You're certain?"

"Positive—I even held the door for her when she left." The lock snapped and the door opened about two inches.

"You wouldn't lie to me?" he asked quietly.

" 'Course not. She's gone."

Trevor Brannigan, heroic war correspondent, slowly opened the door and stepped out of the bathroom. There's no air conditioning in the bathroom, and he was dripping with perspiration. Even his cigar looked sweaty. Bran seemed awfully sheepish.

"I hear the presses—did Mitch get back?" I shook my head. "Then who did page one?" I told him I had and he looked even more sheepish. I followed him to the newsroom and he went directly to his desk. One of the young guys who works in the back shop brings copies of the *Chronicle* up to the newsroom just as soon as the paper comes off the press. That way, if there are any terrible mistakes, we have a chance to catch them right away, stop the presses and make the corrections. Bran picked up the fresh *Chronicle* on his desk and studied it, frowning, and I sat down at my desk and pretended not to watch him. Finally he spoke.

"Not bad," he said, looking over at me. "Fact, it's a good-looking page, Mark."

"Matt," I said.

He ignored my correction. "Maybe you'd better forget about marine biology, after all," he said. "Looks as though you have the makings of a newsman." He said it casually, like he was commenting on the weather, yet it was about the greatest compliment I had ever received. I could feel my face getting red and I stumbled a thank-you.

"No, kid, *I* should be thanking *you*. You kept that Fitzamajig woman off my back and, on top of everything, put together a sharp-looking page one. Much obliged, Mark."

"Matt," I said, and he nodded. "What is it with you and that woman?"

Bran shook his head and dropped into his chair. "The old biddy's a grass widow—divorced—and for some wild reason I'll never comprehend, she has it in her mind that she wants to marry *me*. I think she loves me, of all things. Ten minutes with her and I'm ready to start banging my head against the wall." He leaned back in his swivel chair and planted his heels on the desk.

"That buzzer. . . ."

"It's my first line of defense. I have the business office

trained to signal me the minute that woman sets foot in this building. Sometimes she manages to sneak past them, but not often.

"Trevor! Can you imagine that? She calls me *Trevor!* Nobody's called me that since my seventh birthday, except for a sweet old maiden auntie, rest her soul, and I never could break her of the habit."

I laughed.

"Come on," he said, swinging his feet to the floor. "I owe you a lunch."

I think Bran was more interested in having me scout for him than in having my company for lunch. I felt like some kind of a spy, or something. First of all I stuck my head out the front door and made certain the street was clear—meaning that Mrs. Fitzhugh was nowhere to be seen—and then I signaled him to come ahead.

It was like that all the way over to the Crandall House, with Bran hiding in doorways, stepping into alleyways, walking close to the buildings. I had to go into the hotel first, check the lobby, then give him the all-clear sign. Instead of having lunch in the fancy dining room or the coffee shop, we ate in the bar—where all the rich cattlemen gather to talk and drink—even though neither of us had anything stronger to drink than iced tea. It was dark in there and Bran made certain we got a table off in a far corner. The bar was one place Bran was fairly certain Mrs. Fitzhugh would never set foot. It was safe territory for him.

Over lunch I kept trying to steer the conversation to the subject of World War II, hoping Bran would tell me about some of his experiences as a correspondent.

"I've read your books," I told him. "Both of them, and they were really great." Bran nodded and sort of half-smiled and went on eating. I guessed he must get tired of having people tell him that. When he didn't answer, I said, "What was it like, Bran? Covering the war, I mean?"

Swallowing, he frowned. "That was a long time ago and I've written a lot of stories since then," he said. "I've put millions of words through the typewriter since that war ended, Mark.

"Now, when I look back on those days I don't remember the good things—there weren't many good things, but there were a few. Instead, I remember all those young lives that ended so abruptly and tragically and I think about what those young lives might've become if they'd had a chance. Looking back I realize there was nothing romantic, nothing glamorous about those times, Mark. I find myself remembering only the pain and suffering and fear and madness—all things I'd as soon forget."

"I'm sorry," I told him. "I wouldn't have mentioned it if—"

"Don't be sorry—a good newsman's got to ask questions. It's just that I'd rather not answer any of them about the war, Mark. The dashing young correspondent—that's a part of me that doesn't exist any longer. That guy who said war is hell—he was right.

"But thanks," he said, picking up his sandwich again. "I'm glad you liked the books."

After a while the conversation got going again, but just rambled aimlessly, in no particular direction. Mostly the talk was about the *Chronicle* and Crandall and reporting and Mrs. Fitzhugh. He bristled when I mentioned the woman's name.

"You just can't get away from that woman," Bran said, and he bit savagely into his bacon, lettuce and tomato sandwich. "She's managed to become the publicity chairman of half the groups in town, and for a while she was spending more time in the newsroom than I was."

Bran told me how she kept inviting him over to her house for dinner and to dances and teas and church socials. "Me," he said. "Can you imagine me at a church social?"

Both of us laughed. "So you've got a groupie," I said, "just like the rock stars."

"She's more like a pain in the ass than a groupie," he insisted. When we were finished eating we went back to the office and spent the afternoon working there and then that evening Shan was going to clean her room, so I didn't bicycle out to the Garritys' place. Instead I went down to the police station and asked the desk sergeant to radio Tomas to pick me up there if he felt like having some company on patrol. He did.

It was quiet that night riding around with Tomas. The citizens of Crandall were behaving themselves, so we had plenty of time to talk. He had been born and raised in Crandall, he told me that night, and he talked about how he had gone up to the University of Arizona at Tucson and got his degree there, but instead of going to some big city to get a high-paying job, he had decided to come back to Crandall.

"This is my life here," he said. "My people have lived in this area since before there *was* a Crandall—since before it was part of the United States, in fact. It's home. From way back, our men have always been miners. Me, I'm the first one in my family to go to college, and I'm determined not to be the last. And I keep thinking maybe I can do some good around here."

"You think you'll be a policeman all your life?" I asked.

"Who knows?" he answered. "I can think of a worse way to earn a living. Maybe some day I'll even make chief, if old Blueford ever decides to retire. 'Course, by that time I'd probably be ready to retire myself. He expects to go on being chief of police forever."

Tomas was easy to be with, and I enjoyed riding with him. He was in his mid-twenties, but in some ways he seemed lots younger. I think it was his cool, casual way that made him seem so. He got along well with the kids in Crandall, and I never heard any of them call him a "pig," nor did any of the older people call him Officer Duarte. It was always just "Tomas."

He had dark hair that was thick and wavy and eyes that were dark brown, but not quite as dark as mine. Usually he wore a grin on his handsome face, but when trouble came along the grin disappeared and he was all business. Just one look at his shoulders and arms was enough to make anyone think twice before tangling with him, and I imagine he was awfully fast on his feet. He always looked as though he was ready to take off running.

For a while that evening we rode the streets, neither of us talking, just keeping our eyes open. Occasionally Tomas flashed the spotlight up alleys, behind bushes, on rooftops. Then we did some door shaking. At least that's what the police call it. We got out of the patrol car and walked along Copper Avenue, trying the front doors of the stores and offices, "shaking" them, to make certain they had been locked up for the night. When we were back in the car and moving again, I asked Tomas what he knew about illegal alien smuggling.

"Whoa, horse," he said, "that's a little out of my line. Don't know a whole lot—mostly just what I've read in the papers and magazines. That and what my border-patrol buddies have told me. It's a problem, that's for sure, but it's not in our jurisdiction, so I'm not really all that up on it."

"If I ask you something, Tom—Tomas—will you promise not to laugh at me?"

"Cop's honor," he said. "Ask away."

"Well, it's more telling than asking," I said, correcting myself. And then I told him how I had gone snipe hunting that first night in Crandall, and about how I had tangled with those two Mexican men. I told him the whole story, not leaving out any of the details.

Tomas didn't laugh, not even about the snipe hunt. In fact he seemed really interested. "Got a friend I'd like you to tell that story to," he said when I had finished. "Would you be willing to talk to him?"

"Is he a policeman?"

"Federal," said Tomas. "He's border patrol—guy about my age, sharp. A little eager maybe, but not overly so. You'll like him."

So I told Tomas I'd talk to his friend and asked him when. "How about now, if he's not busy?" I said sure, and Tomas pulled the cruiser into a gas station—it was closed for the night—and made a phone call from the booth on the corner. He was back in the car in less than a minute.

"Wally's expecting us," Tomas said, as he put the car in gear.

13

IT WAS A few minutes after 10 o'clock when we pulled up in the front of a small, neat tract house in one of the newer subdivisions out on the northwest side. Tomas cut the headlights but left the engine running because of the radio, and we sat in the darkness. We didn't have to wait more than a minute before Wally Sternaman came out of the front door and bounded down the walk, buttoning a sport shirt. He was wearing a pair of washed-out Levi's and on his feet were plastic thong sandals. I reached behind me and lifted the lock button on the rear door and he climbed in.

Tomas made the introductions and Wally and I shook hands, and then Tomas flipped on the headlights and we pulled away from the curb. The border patrolman had a big shock of blond hair that looked like it would be a lot of trouble to keep combed, and his mouth was large and overflowed with straight, white teeth.

"This better be worth something, Tomas," he grumbled from the back seat. "Patty was just dishing out ice cream—we always have a bowl of ice cream and watch the 10 o'clock news when I'm not working."

"You federal guys are spoiled, horse," Tomas Duarte

said. "Imagine, a dish of ice cream, the 10 o'clock news and then bedtime. You should put in a stint with the city cops and see what the real world is like."

"The *real* world? Crandall? Tomas, you know better than that. Crandall is as far removed from the real world as a man can get. You've got as cushy a job as any law-enforcement officer could ever hope to have. Face it, you're spoiled."

Tomas laughed. "Well, we'd better not get into that now. I go off shift at midnight and we could go on with this discussion for hours and not get anywhere. Matt, why don't you tell the Ice Cream Kid your story?"

I turned sideways in the seat with my back against the door and, for the second time that night, told my story. "Snipe hunting?" Wally interrupted. "You fell for that?" I admitted that I had and he chuckled, then apologized and told me to go ahead. For the next five minutes I talked without any more interruptions from the border patrolman, except for an occasional "okay," "uh-huh," "hmmmm," and "yeah, go on." All the while Tomas sat behind the wheel of the patrol car, driving the quiet streets of Crandall, shining the spotlight occasionally, checking out his beat.

When I finished, Wally was silent for a few minutes, then finally said, "It fits."

"What do you mean?" I asked.

"Your story—it fits in with what we know," he said. "We have been—" and then he stopped abruptly. "You say you're a reporter for the *Chronicle*, Matt?"

"Right."

"Well, if I give you some background—off the record,

as you newspaper guys say—will you sit on it for the time being? I wouldn't want what I'm about to tell you to get into print until the time is right. It might blow a big one we're working on."

I told Wally I wouldn't write anything until they had finished their investigation and I had cleared it with him. I wanted to hear what he had to say and it was worth the promise for me to get more background information on what was happening.

"You think it's okay to tell him, Tomas?" he asked, and Tomas Duarte nodded. "You can trust Matt," he said. Hearing Tomas say that made me feel good.

"Okay, then. For the last couple of months we've known about an alien smuggling ring working this area," Wally began. "Near as we can tell, it's one of the biggest operations of the sort along the border here. These people are dealing in hundreds of aliens each month."

I whistled. "How do you know all this?" I asked.

"We have people down in Mexico—informants—who have tipped us on it. They tell us that there's a regular network, making contacts down in the interior of Mexico, transporting the illegals up to La Pizca, and then keeping them hidden somewhere over there across the line.

"'Course, even if we knew where they were hiding them over there, there's nothing we could do about it. They're still in Mexico. Only when they set foot in the United States can we make a move against them.

"Well, anyway, Matt, the coyotes—the smugglers, that is—move their people across the border just about any place they care to. That fence is like a sieve. It's chain link along the stretch between Crandall and Pizca, and for a short distance east and west away from the towns. After that though, for several miles each way, it's just five strands of barbed wire. Cattle fence is all it is. Beyond that—nothing but an imaginary line.

"They'll cut that chain link and move their people through there one time, and snip the barbed wire in another place the next time. Once in a while they'll even go out beyond the barbed wire, but they're bold, so they don't often bother to take those precautions. They know we're undermanned and they know how we operate, so they call the shots."

"What happens when illegals get across into this country then?" I asked.

"Well, the coyotes working on this side make the pickup. You said you heard a truck—well, chances are that truck left the place where you were snipe hunting, loaded with a human cargo. This is where we get a little fuzzy on our details.

"Our informants tell us that the coyotes keep their customers under wraps somewhere fairly close to the border for a short time, then move them northward, up to the interstate, and transfer them to another vehicle of some sort that moves them even further north, either east or west. They even provide them with forged identity documents. After that they just disappear in some big city—L.A., Chicago, New York—you name it."

I asked Wally if he knew who any of the smugglers were.

"Not really," he said. "They're a slick bunch—one of the slickest, believe me. Oh, there are a couple of characters we think might be connected with this operation, but we don't have anything really solid on any of them. Besides, they're just the little guys. At this point we're just laying low, waiting for them to make some mistake. We aren't interested in getting just those little guys.

"At the head of all this there's a biggie, and he's the hombre we'd like to grab. He's *numero uno*, and he's sharp as hell. He's the guy who makes it all work, and once we get the make on him, we wipe out the whole operation."

"Do you have a lot of people working on this case?" I asked.

"Ha! That's our problem. We're understaffed here in the Crandall sector. Barely twenty people, and just doing the routine stuff keeps us busy." Then Wally spotted a drive-in. "Ice cream cones—pull in, Tomas. I'll buy."

So Tomas Duarte wheeled off the street onto the drive-in's parking apron. Wally asked both of us what flavors we wanted, then ran into the place, his sandals flapping on the pavement. He was back in a couple of minutes, juggling three ice cream cones. He passed two of them through the window to us, took a lick at his own scoop of chocolate before it dripped, then asked Tomas for two dollars.

"Funny thing happened to me on the way to your patrol car," he said. "Hurried so to get some clothes on that I plumb forgot my wallet." Tomas sighed and handed me his cone to hold while he fished the bills from his wallet.

"And make sure you bring me the change," he hollered

after Wally's floppy sandals. When the border patrolman was in the back seat again we stayed parked for a few minutes until Tomas finished his cone, and then we were back patrolling again.

"Now, where were we?" asked Wally.

"You were bitching about how overworked you are," Tomas answered.

"Right," said the border patrolman. "We have people patrolling the line in jeeps, we use planes, when we can we set up electronic sensing devices—you name it, we do it. But our sector takes in a lot of border, and we can't have people everywhere at once."

Tomas nodded. "I know—you could line up an army shoulder to shoulder along that border," he put in, "and a guy would still get through."

Wally agreed. "We get this outfit though, and we've got a big one. It's taking us a while, but one of these days we'll break it." For a few seconds he was quiet while he crunched on the cone, then he asked me if I had anything to add to what I had told him.

"Nothing I can think of right now."

"Do you remember exactly where it was you had the hassle with those guys?"

"Not the *exact* place," I said slowly. "Only thing I know for sure is that it's somewhere out west of town. Way out in the boonies." I told Wally I'd find out from Shannon exactly where it had been and then let him know.

Great, he said, and then he reminded me not to write anything about what he had told me and I promised I wouldn't. "And one more thing—don't tell anybody you've been talking to me about this, and for that matter, I wouldn't spread it around, if I were you, about what happened to you on the snipe hunt. Okay?"

"Okay," I agreed, "but if this story breaks before I leave here at the end of the summer, I sure want to be the one to write it."

"A deal," he promised.

We pulled up in front of Wally's house and he climbed out of the car. "Thanks for the ride," he said, leaning down to talk through my open window, "and Tomas— thanks for the ice cream cone." Then he raised his hand to me. "See you, Matt," and he turned and flip-flopped up the sidewalk to his front door.

When Tomas dropped me off at the Railroad Hotel it was almost midnight and I was really beat, but I had plenty to do before I went to bed. I undressed, wrapped a big towel around my middle and hurried down the hallway and took a shower. When I returned to the room I sat cross-legged on the bed and in the big notebook that I had used to make notes from the clippings and articles in the *Chronicle*'s file, I wrote down everything I could remember about what Wally had told me. I knew that if I waited until the next day I might forget some of it, and I wanted to get it all down while it was fresh in my mind.

By the time I was ready to turn out the lights it was after one-thirty, and I was so sleepy I could hardly keep my eyes propped open. I wound my alarm clock, dreading the thought of getting up at six o'clock—I had to be at the office at seven—and so I cheated and set it for six-fifteen, telling myself I'd just hurry a little more than usual in the morning.

But beat as I was, I couldn't go to sleep right away. I lay thinking about everything Wally had told me, and about all I had read about smuggling illegal aliens, and I was trying to think of what I should do next in my own part of the investigation, and the feeling came to me that there was something I wasn't remembering about that night of the snipe hunt. I couldn't put my finger on just what it was and it sort of nibbled away at my mind.

Finally though, I did drop off to sleep. I dragged myself out of bed at six-fifteen, and the thought was still there in my mind that I was forgetting something about that night.

14

THAT DAY TURNED out to be a very special one for me. I covered the most important story I'd been assigned all summer, and ended up with a big story on page one, complete with my first by-line, such as it was.

Usually I'm not a coffee drinker—I like milk a lot better—but once in a while I have a cup just because newspaper people are always drinking coffee in the movies I've seen and the books I've read. I figured that if I was going to be a newsman, I'd have to get used to drinking coffee. That morning I was feeling so draggy and cobwebby that I had a stack of pancakes for breakfast and then washed it all down with a couple cups of coffee. Black, even, which is how both Mitch and Bran drink it. I was a bit wider awake when I unchained the bike from the lamppost next to the Railroad Hotel and almost felt human as I pedaled over to the police station, as I did every morning to make an early check on the reports from the night before.

The minute I walked into the station, Captain Joe Moreno called me over to his desk. "Message here for you, Matt," he said. "Garrity called and said for you to get your ass into the office on the double." I thanked him and hurried to the bike.

Pedaling toward the *Chronicle* building I realized that Mitch might've said for me to *hurry* to the office, but the part about getting my *ass* there on the double had to be the captain's interpretation of the message. I looked at my watch—it was ten minutes to seven as I locked the bike to the drainpipe next to the loading dock behind the paper. I hurried upstairs.

"Morning, Matt," said Mitch. "We have a problem here—hope you can help us out."

They had just had a phone call from the sheriff's department that a freight train had derailed on the main line, about fifteen or twenty miles north of Crandall.

"We've got to cover it—pictures and story—of course, but the problem is, I've got to be up in Tucson for a state press association meeting at one o'clock," said Mitch. "That means I've got to leave here by ten-thirty. Think you could handle the derailment story, Matt?"

Could I! "Sure," I said. "Bran checked me out with the old Speed Graphic a couple of weeks ago, and I've shot quite a few pics since then and—" I stopped short and I know my face clouded over.

"Something wrong, Mark?" asked Bran, looking up from his typewriter.

"Yeah," I said. "It would take me forever to pedal up there and back on that old bicycle."

Both of them laughed. "Consider that problem solved," Mitch said. "Bran says you can take his car."

"You do have a license, don't you?" Bran asked. I told him sure, since the day I turned sixteen. "And you're a pretty good driver?" I said I thought I was. Bran nodded and went back to his typing.

Mitch said he wanted to send me so Bran could stay in the office to work desk. He'd back up Bran and make the police and fire checks and write those stories before he headed for Tucson. It made me feel good to know they had enough confidence in me to have me cover a big story.

On the large county map on the wall, Mitch showed me how to get to the location of the accident, and then gave me a few tips on questions to ask the officials at the scene of the wreck.

"Think you can handle it, son?" he asked.

"Sure—at least I'll do my best."

"Can't ask for more than that," said Mitch, and then he clapped a hand on my shoulder and let it rest there for a second.

I grabbed the old Speed Graphic from the supply closet, checked the bag to make certain the film holders were loaded, made sure I had a couple of ballpoint pens in my pocket and then folded up about a dozen sheets of copy paper into a big wad and jammed it into my hip pocket. "Guess that's everything," I said, looking around.

Standing up, Bran dug down into his pocket for the keys. "You know which car is mine?"

"That yellow-orange Maverick parked out behind?"

"That's the one," he said, handing me the car keys. "She might be just a Maverick, but she's got the soul of a Mercedes. Treat her well and she'll get you there and back."

Grabbing the camera, I headed for the stairs. "And

Matt," Mitch called after me. I stopped on the top step and turned to him.

"Yes?" I said.

"Be careful, son," he told me. "Don't take any chances. The story's not *that* important." I grinned at him and waved, tromping down the stairs. He sounded just like my dad. I guess all fathers are forever telling their kids to be careful.

It turned out to be a little over twenty-four miles up to the scene of the wreck. I went out the Tucson highway, then north on the road to Corinth. Just short of the side road to Mitch's ranch I passed Jess Perry in his big new truck, and tooted my horn and gave him a wave. He was headed toward Crandall and he must not have recognized me because he didn't so much as honk back. About four miles past the Garrity ranch I turned east on an unpaved county road and followed it for a few miles, then turned north again on another back road and after a while came to a narrow cow path that ran along the main line of the railroad. I heard a deep booming sound, and then, far ahead beyond some hills, I suddenly saw a huge tongue of flame lick upward, then a ball of fire, and finally great clouds of black smoke. I stepped on the accelerator.

As I topped a hill I saw the train and about twenty people and some trucks and sheriff's cars, all well away from the train. I parked Bran's car on top of the hill, grabbed the Graphic, guessed at the exposure, cocked the shutter and started shooting. I made three overall shots of the scene from up there, and decided to save the rest of the film in case I could get some close-up shots later. Then I quickly jotted some notes about what I saw. As I hurried downhill toward the train, I stopped to talk with a deputy sheriff. I told him who I was and asked about the explosion.

"Propane," he said. "That explosion a few minutes ago? That was the second one that blew. I wouldn't get any closer, if I was you. Three more tank cars there, all loaded with propane."

"Any idea what caused the derailment?"

"I've heard some talk," the deputy said. "Might have been a problem with the track, according to some people, or maybe a mechanical breakdown on one of the cars. Won't know for sure until the investigators get here and have a look and issue their official statement."

Carefully I made notes of what the deputy told me and wrote down his name and then asked about the crew.

"Four men, all safe. No fatalities, no injuries, thank God, and nearly as we can tell, no one was riding any of the freight cars. We checked before the first propane tanker went up."

I thanked the deputy and poked around some more, and then I talked with the engineer. He seemed shaken, and told me he couldn't talk to me—not until the railroad officials turned up on the scene.

"All's I can tell you, sonny, is that one minute we was on the tracks—the next we wasn't. It's just as simple as that." A woman from one of the ranches in the area came up and handed the engineer a cup of coffee, and he thanked her and sat on a rock and gazed down at what had been his train.

Both of the diesels were still standing on the rails, as

were the first three cars behind them. From there on, for about fifteen or twenty cars back, it was just one big, twisted mess, with plenty of fire.

My ballpoint flew across the copy paper as I tried to get everything down. Then I made a few photos of the engineer sitting on the rock drinking coffee, and then went as close to the train as the deputies would let me, and took more pictures.

When I thought I had everything I could get at the scene, I trotted back to the car, climbed in and headed back to Crandall.

As I drove I tried to put the story together in my mind, as I would write it. I tried to think of a good lead sentence or paragraph that would tie it all together; the most important facts—the details that our readers would want to know first.

Instead of going right to the office, I drove to the camera shop that processes all the *Chronicle*'s film. Charlie Prentiss, the owner, said I could use his type-writer while he developed my film and made prints. As he went into the darkroom, I telephoned the office.

Bran picked up the phone on the second ring. "I'm at Charlie's place," I said. "Should have some good shots and a pretty decent story." Quickly I told him about the accident and described the pictures I had taken.

"You coming back to the office right away to do the story?"

"I thought I'd stand by here and write the story on Charlie's typewriter and bring the pics with me when they're printed."

That sounded like a good idea, he said. "If the

negatives look good, have Charlie print the overall shot four columns wide and about eight inches deep, and the one of the engineer drinking coffee—have him make it two columns, maybe six inches deep. And about the story, Mark, think you can write four takes?"

A take is a page. I didn't even bother trying to correct him on my name. "I can do four takes without any problem," I told him.

"Good. I'll write the head and cutlines from what you've told me, and I'll block out the story for four takes and the pics for the sizes I told you. Get the copy and photos over here as quickly as you can."

I went into the little office at the rear of the shop, sat down at the desk, put a piece of Prentiss Photo Studio stationery into the typewriter and started banging away.

"Four railroad crewmen escaped injury this morning when. . . ."

I got it all in, all the details, all the facts, all the quotes, all the color. I was just about to put the ### marks at the bottom of the fourth page to show that was the end of the story, when Charlie came out of the darkroom with the prints.

I took a quick look at the photos and was pleased—thrilled, really—with what I saw. The focus was sharp, they had the right contrast, there was plenty of action. No editor could have asked for more.

Within minutes I was in the newsroom. Bran grabbed a quick look at the pictures, then told me to put them on the engraving machine and start it running. He settled down at his desk with the copy and I collapsed into my chair. It had been a wild morning and I was still running on high. Bran finished reading copy on the piece, dropped it down the chute and came over to my desk.

"Good story, Mark," he said to me. "Maybe not great, but damn good. Couldn't have done better myself." He looked at the clock. "It's about lunchtime—why don't you run over and get yourself an early bite. You've earned it."

He didn't have to make the offer twice. I was walking on air, yet I was ready for some food. A lot had happened since I downed those pancakes and two cups of coffee that morning.

Downstairs I asked Shannon if she could get away for an early lunch and she thought so. "I'll meet you at the Sugar Bowl in about ten minutes if I can. You go ahead and order, though. Don't wait for me."

I didn't. I ordered the special burger in a basket, a side of coleslaw and a chocolate shake. Shan came in even before the waitress had brought my food, and after she ordered I told her all about my morning.

"And wait until you see the pictures," I told her. "They're fantastic, even if I say so myself." I was still riding high; I couldn't help it. Shan seemed just as pleased about the story as I was. It was great to have someone like her to share it with.

Through the meal we talked, and then we talked some more when we were finished eating. "I'd like to take a ride tonight," I said. "Out west of town. Think you can get the car?"

Shan raised her eyebrows. "Now, just *what* do you

have in mind, young man?" she asked. "I thought you knew—I'm not *that* kind of a girl!"

"You mean all this time you've just been leading me on?" I asked.

"Me? Leading *you* on? Why, you've been pursuing me since the evening you hit town!"

"That's exactly what I had in mind," I said. "I'd like you to show me just where you took me snipe hunting that evening I did hit town."

"Gee, Winky, here I thought you were getting romantic ideas."

"No such luck, Miss Garrity. Strictly in the line of business."

"You mean part of your 'investigation'?"

"Exactly. I'd like to return to the scene of the crime, as they say."

"You really know how to hurt a girl, don't you. Well, that's kind of a letdown, but I suppose I can arrange it. Seven o'clock?"

I told her seven would be fine, and then I looked up at the clock. "Come on," I said, standing up and tugging on her arm. "The presses should have been running for ten minutes, at least. I'm anxious to see my story."

We paid and then hurried back to the office. I almost had to drag her. Sometimes girls pick the worst times to be pokey.

My copy of the Crandall *Chronicle* was there on my desk waiting for me. Bran was talking on the phone. I sat down, unfolded the paper and spread it out in front of me. The photos reproduced beautifully, and above them,

the two-line banner headline said, "FAULTY EQUIP-
MENT OR TRACK MAY HAVE CAUSED DERAIL-
MENT," and it led to a two-column head about the
propane tankers exploding. I felt a funny sort of thrill
come over me, complete with the hair on my neck
prickling out.

Then my eyes dropped a little bit lower and took in my
very first by-line on a real newspaper:

By Mark Althaus
Chronicle Staff Writer

Mark!
It was like somebody had hit me in the gut with a ball
bat. My first by-line and it had my name wrong! I
wanted to cry or scream or pound on my desk, or
something. Then Bran got off the phone.

"Bran!" I hollered. "My name is *Matt*! Matt for
Matthew, not Mark! This by-line—it says *Mark* Althaus
wrote the story and he didn't. *I* did! Me—*Matt* Althaus.
I wrote it, Bran, I wrote it!" I was so mad I was close to
tears.

"Sorry, kid," he apologized. "We caught it after a
couple of dozen papers had run off. Stopped the press
right away and made the fix. The rest of the run has your
name right." He handed me a copy of the *Chronicle* with
the corrected by-line in it.

I let out a deep breath and then began to laugh and
Bran laughed with me. Then he got up and said he was
going to lunch, and asked me to hold down the fort until
he got back.

At the top of the steps he paused and looked back at

me. "Sorry about the mistake," he said, "but it was a damn fine story, Mark."

I flung my copy of that afternoon's *Chronicle* at him—the one that said *Mark*—but I missed. Bran was still laughing when he went out the front door.

I laughed too. It could've been worse. The by-line could've said: By *Winky* Althaus!

15

FOR TWO NIGHTS I played detective. Well, sort of detective. The first night was more fun, because Shan was with me. The second night turned out to be nowhere near as pleasant.

At seven o'clock on the evening of the train derailment, Shan picked me up and we drove west, out of town. "Do you think you can remember where we were that night?"

"I think so," she said. "At least pretty close to it."

It took only about twenty minutes to drive out to where they had left the car that night, and Shannon parked the yellow wagon in the same place. We got out of the car and started hiking southward, toward Mexico. The sun was still well above the mountains to the west, so we had enough daylight left for poking around.

"I really think it was right around here that we started the hunt," she said thoughtfully, as we topped a hill.

Looking around I didn't see anything that looked at all familiar. Wherever you looked, it was all cactus and mesquite and paloverde trees and rocks and sand. Lots of sand. It all looked the same to me.

With hands on hips I turned looking in every direction. "If this is the right place," I said to her, "then when you all left me to chase the snipe my way, you went in that direction, isn't that right?" I pointed toward a distant rise.

Shan said that was the way they had gone. "And then we went straight ahead, beyond the next couple of hills, then doubled back through a deep arroyo, toward the car. It's a wonder you didn't hear us when we started the engine and drove off."

"I guess I was so busy concentrating on the hunting that I didn't hear anything." I gave her a disgusted look, then I squatted down. "It was right about here then, that I waited, holding that silly pillowcase and flashlight."

Shan came and stood behind me and put her hands on my shoulders and worked her fingers in my muscles. It felt great. "You really fell for it, Winky. I couldn't believe that you were so gullible." Her voice was soft and the way she said it, it didn't sound as though she was teasing me. Not much, at least.

"And then," I said as I stood up, "I started wandering."

"Which way did you go?"

"Oh, boy, don't ask me that. Here, there, everywhere. I have no sense of direction. I get lost in my own bedroom."

So we started walking. No place in particular, just wandering, the way I had on that night. I draped an arm

over Shannon's shoulder and she hung her thumb on the
back belt loop of my Levi's. When we got to the top of
another hill, we stopped again.

"Now, where's the border from here? I'm all turned
around."

"That way," she said, gesturing with her free hand.
"Probably half a mile. Do you want to go down there?"

"Is there anything to see?"

"Barbed wire and more cactus. The Mexican side of
the border looks exactly the same as the U. S. side."

"Then we might as well save our energy. I had
thought about looking for tire tracks off the road where
the truck had made the pickup, but that heavy rain we
had that night would have washed away any signs."

So we turned and started toward the car. By then the
sun had dropped behind the mountains and daylight was
fading fast. There were quite a few clouds in the sky and
they were beginning to pick up the sunset colors, and we
came to an outcropping of rock on top of one of the hills
and decided to sit down and enjoy the sunset.

With our backs against a boulder, we relaxed and
watched the reds and oranges as they deepened and
played on the clouds. It was a real show, like a skyful of
fireworks on the Fourth of July, only more so. It was the
kind of picture you see in *Arizona Highways* magazine,
except that this was live, and not on paper. For what
must have been at least fifteen minutes we sat watching,
hardly talking at all.

One of us would notice a cloud that looked like a purple
pig, or one that was shaped like a pink castle, and we'd
point out those formations to each other, but except for

that, we sat quietly. I had my arm around Shan and she had curled up close and we were happy just watching the sky together. Just sharing it. It was almost as if it belonged to us alone, as if it were our own private sunset. There weren't even any interruptions for commercials.

When almost all of the color had drained from the sky, Shan lifted her face and kissed me on the cheek.

"How much time?" she asked. "Three weeks?"

"How much time for what?"

"Until you leave, stupey. Until you go home."

"About that," I said. "Three weeks and a couple of days."

"I'll miss you, Winky. I really will."

"You'll write?"

"I said before I would. My letters will probably bore you silly, but I'll write."

"You'll have to let me know what's going on down here. I've really gotten to like Crandall."

"Oh, now don't expect all that. If you want to know what's going on down here you'll just have to get a mail subscription to the *Chronicle*. I don't want to write *that* sort of thing."

"Then what will you write?" I asked her.

"Oh, I don't know. Maybe about a mean little boy named Winky, who I used to know when I was a little girl. I'd write about how I hated him because he was so nasty to me."

She laughed softly. "And then I'd write about how that mean little boy grew up to be a—" Shan paused.

"Go ahead. Grew up to be a what?"

"Oh, I don't know," she teased. "I haven't really

decided yet just what he grew up to be. I'm still thinking about it."

"You better think fast. Three weeks. . . ."

"I know," Shannon said. "This summer has gone so fast and I haven't done much of anything with all my friends—the kids I've known all my life. I haven't wanted to—I've just wanted to be with you."

I tried to think of something to say to her then that would let her know I felt the same way, but I just couldn't come up with the right words. So I brought her face up to mine and I kissed her. She got the message. Her cheek was wet.

"You're crying," I said, and she shrugged.

"It's the sunset," she answered, clearing her throat. "Sunsets do that to me. Sunsets and weddings and graduations." She tried to laugh, but it didn't work. "Winky, you've made this summer so wonderful—it's been like no other summer—but I'm going to miss you *so* much."

We kissed again and then I held her close to me for a few minutes. After a while she cleared her throat again and said we'd better be going back to town. "Mom's all alone tonight because Daddy won't get back from Tucson until late. I promised her I wouldn't be out long. I'm sorry, Winky."

We stood and kissed one more time and then, holding hands, walked slowly back to the car. We didn't talk much. We didn't have to because we both knew how the other felt.

Next night when I played detective again, it didn't work out quite that way. Not by a long shot, it didn't.

On my way to the police station to check reports first

thing the next morning, I stopped at an outdoor phone booth in front of the city building, where I was sure no one could hear me, and telephoned Wally at his home. I told him that Shan had driven me out to the snipe-hunt site the night before, and I was able to give him fairly accurate directions to the spot. He thanked me and said he'd see me around.

When I went to the office that morning, I took my spiral with all the illegal alien notes in it. I wanted to type up all the information so I'd have it in better form, so I'd be able to use the notes more easily. Whenever I had a few minutes I pecked away at it, and because it was a slow day, I got several pages done.

Late in the afternoon Bran paused at my desk as he walked toward the steps. "Hope that story you're working on so industriously isn't for tomorrow's paper, Mark. It'll be a small edition and already it's crowded with ads," he said.

I had given up trying to make him remember that my name was Matt. "It's not," I said. "It's just some notes I'm typing up for a story I might write some day, or maybe might never write, for that matter."

Trevor Brannigan leaned over my typewriter and had a look at what I was typing. I couldn't keep him from it.

"Hmmmm, illegal aliens." Then he straightened up and looked toward me. "Didn't know you were assigned to do a piece about illegals," he said.

"Well, I wasn't. Mostly what I'm doing is just sort of—you know, playing around with it. Practice, call it. It's just something I'm a little interested in. Maybe this fall I'll write a term paper about it for social studies." I hoped that would satisfy him so that he would move along and forget about me. He didn't. He seemed interested.

"What angle are you taking?" he asked.

"I'm not even that far yet. I'm just putting some notes together, is what I'm doing."

"That's a pretty sticky subject, Mark. Some strong feelings here in town about alien smuggling—both for and against. You'd best watch yourself."

"Oh, I wouldn't do anything to get in trouble," I told him. "You sure don't have to worry about that."

For a few seconds he frowned, looking at me thoughtfully through his glasses. Bran nodded then, but he didn't seem really satisfied by what I said.

"Well then, you be careful what you get into, Mark, hear?"

"I hear," I said, and he put his unlit cigar into his mouth and turned and went down the stairs.

It bothered me that Bran would take that sort of an attitude, but I shook it off. I didn't have time to worry about such things just then. I typed two more paragraphs and decided I'd done enough work for that day. Besides, I had big plans for the evening and things to do to get ready, so I put the spiral and my typed notes into a large manila envelope, tucked it into my drawer and went downstairs to see Miss Garrity.

Much as I hated to, especially after the great way things had gone with us the night before, I told Shannon that I had some things I had to take care of that evening, so I wouldn't be able to see her. I was really torn about it, because I'd much rather have been with her than doing what I had planned, but the days were running out for me and if I was going to try to get to the bottom of the smuggling story, I had to hustle. On my way to the hotel I stopped at the hardware store and bought a flashlight and some batteries, and right after dinner I climbed onto the old green bicycle and started pedaling out toward the place Shan and I had visited the night before.

It had been much easier and much more pleasant riding in the air-conditioned station wagon with Shan. I had been using the bike to get around town quite a bit, so I was used to it, but it was a long haul out to the snipe-hunting grounds and that bike wasn't easy to pump. Besides that, it was hot. It was always hot in Arizona. Before I was halfway there I was dripping with sweat and my legs felt like they were ready to fall off, and by the time I *did* get there and had the bike stashed in a clump of bushes, my legs were numb and I wasn't any too sure whether they'd hold me up. It was almost as if they were made of rubber.

After I was on my feet for a few minutes they began to behave and they started carrying me in the direction of the border fence. The sun was almost ready to disappear beyond the mountains and I knew I didn't have too much daylight left. At first what I wanted to do was walk the border for a distance to get a good idea of what it looked like so I'd be able to describe it if ever I did write an alien smuggling story. Oh, I'd look around for clues or signs of some sort, too, but I didn't actually expect to come across anything that would help me after so much time had passed.

Before long I went over a low hill and about a hundred yards ahead was the fence. As Shan had said, it wasn't much. Just five strands of barbed wire stretched between steel posts. So much for that. I didn't want to get too close to the fence because for a distance of twelve or fifteen feet on the United States' side of it, it had been dragged.

Tomas Duarte had told me about how the border patrol people would attach a "drag" made of chains to the back of a jeep and then haul it along the cleared strip just inside the fence. Later they would go back and check the strip, looking for footprints in the drag that would tell them someone had jumped the fence there and had come into this country illegally. I sure didn't want my footprints messing up the strip, so I kept clear of it.

For maybe half a mile I walked along the rough ground staying about a hundred feet away from the fence, until I found a likely looking spot. There were some good-sized hills right there, and a deep arroyo, or gully, that ran among them, and if I were a Mexican wanting to jump the fence, I'd probably look for a place just like that.

It was beginning to get dark when I settled down there in a little draw that cut between two of the hills. There were some creosote bushes nearby that would hide me, and from that vantage point I had a clear view of a long section of the fence. At least I would until darkness came.

What I had in mind was what they call a "stakeout" on

the TV cop shows. I didn't see why an investigative reporter couldn't stake out something the way a detective did. Of course I actually didn't expect to have anything happen right there where I was—that would be asking too much—but I knew I had to do something and I really didn't know what else to try. So I settled in and waited.

Darkness came before long and in a while I couldn't see much of anything in any direction. I knew that in a while the moon would be up and it would be pretty full that night. In the meantime I sat quietly as I could, just listening. All I heard though, was the occasional yapping and yipping of a far-off coyote. Just sitting there as I was, there wasn't a whole lot else to do, so I let a bunch of thoughts drift in and out of my mind. One minute I found myself thinking about Shan and wishing she were sitting out there with me in the middle of the desert and how much more fun that would be, and the next I was thinking about illegal aliens. It was hard for me to imagine what it must be like to live down in Mexico where so many people were poor, because I've been lucky. I've always lived in a nice home and had decent clothes to wear. My dad works hard and earns a good living, and there's always been plenty to eat. In a way I felt guilty about having such a good life, about never having had to go to bed hungry, or anything, the way a lot of kids do. It wasn't hard to understand why so many Mexican people tried to get into this country where they thought things would be much better for them.

Then I got to thinking about Vicente. I wondered if he had gone back home yet, or if he was still staying with his uncle. I wished I had found out where his uncle lived, because it would have helped me a lot to be able to talk with Vicente about what life was like in Mexico. I mean really like. He could have helped me a lot with my story, I know. I wondered if I should just go across the line some day and ride my bike around, looking for Vicente. Then I laughed to myself. What a stupid thing *that* would be. I'd never find him there—not in a million years.

Then my thoughts were back with Shannon again—I always thought a lot about her—and how I hated the idea of leaving her in just three weeks. The summer had been so perfect that I kept wishing there was some way to make it go on forever, or if not forever, at least for a few more months. At the same time though, I looked forward to getting home and seeing my family again. All summer I'd been too busy to be really homesick, but I had to admit that I missed my folks. I even missed Allison, and she's as pesky as most little sisters are. Then there was school. I was anxious to get back to school in the fall, as silly as that might sound, because it would be my senior year and that would be a lot of fun. And besides, the next year I'd be going away to college and majoring in journalism, and then when I got out of the university I'd get a newspaper job and be a real reporter, not just a kid working on a paper for the summer. But Shan, how I wished she fit into my immediate plans more than just being a pen pal. It was going to be hard to leave her. And Mitch and Aunt Beth, too, for that matter. I felt so close to them that they were like another family to me, except that Mitch and

Beth didn't nag me, the way real parents sometimes do.

I had closed my eyes to rest them and I guess I must have dropped off to sleep. Next thing I knew I jerked awake, hearing the sound of a car or truck or something, coming my way. Out in the middle of nowhere, your ears can play tricks on you, so I wasn't too sure just what I was hearing, or where the sound, whatever it was, actually was coming from. I held my breath and listened carefully. When the car stopped it sounded as if it were a couple of hills away from where I was hidden, but I couldn't be sure. The sound came from behind me, away from the border.

For what seemed like an hour but was probably only ten minutes, I sat absolutely still in my hiding place, afraid even to take a deep breath. I heard nothing else, no other sound. Somebody was out there though, I knew, and I had to find out who it was and what he was up to.

Never in my life had I been as scared as I was just then. I began to wonder how important it was for me to be out there, snooping, and for that matter, how important it was for me to be working on that smuggling story. What good would it do? It was no business of mine. All I had to do was write about ice cream socials and fender benders and bowling tournaments. I didn't have to poke around and expose a big alien smuggling ring. That's not what I was getting paid for. Bran was right. Investigative reporter? Forget it.

But I'd gone that far, I thought, and I'd done all the ground work and I knew I'd never forgive myself if I didn't find out who was doing the smuggling, who was out there prowling around. Before I knew it I had suffered a sudden case of foolish bravery.

Quietly as I could, I began inching out of my hiding place, following the arroyo that cut around the base of those hills. I inched along like a worm on a leaf, keeping low, heading away from the border in the direction of the car sounds I had heard.

Every few feet I would stop and lie still on my front side, just listening. The moon was up now and it helped to be able to see a little. After I had gone about fifty or maybe seventy-five feet I still didn't hear anything, so I began crawling, and after a while I got even braver, and crouching low, I ran in short dashes, from cover to cover.

I had just left the cover of a mesquite tree and was making for a clump of creosote bushes when the voice cut through the quiet.

"*Que pasa?*" it said. Even though it was in Spanish, I got the idea. If there had been a ceiling there I would have gone right through it, I was so scared. But I was almost to the bushes so I kept going. The voice shot out again, and this time I understood it completely.

"*Alto!*" it said, and then in English, "*Freeze*, buddy!"

Believe me, I *froze*.

16

BEFORE I KNEW it I was standing with my palms against the rough bark of a mesquite tree, my feet spread apart, and somebody else's foot hooked just inside my left one, ready to send me sprawling if I made one false move. I didn't, though. The somebody who belonged to that foot patted me down then, like they do in the movies. All he found in the way of weapons was a flashlight, which isn't what you would call lethal. He seemed almost disappointed.

I didn't know what to expect. I had no idea whose prisoner I was, but I suspected I had been captured by a member of the smuggling ring.

"Okay, buddy," said the voice. "You can turn around now—but turn slowly."

I did, keeping my hands sort of half-raised, so I wouldn't give the guy any excuse to shoot me. I'd never met any alien smugglers before, but I imagined they could be a mean lot, considering the line of work they were in. Why, a coyote would just as soon shoot a person as not, and here I had surprised this one right when he was up to who knows what. I was afraid I was in for it. A powerful flashlight beam was shining in my eyes and I couldn't see a thing.

"What's your citizenship?" asked the voice.

"What's my what?"

"Your citizenship," the voice repeated impatiently. "Are you a citizen of the United States?"

"Of course I am," I said, my voice sounding thin and weak.

Then I heard someone crashing through the underbrush behind me. I was surrounded.

"Relax, Thede," came another voice. "The kid's okay."

The second voice sounded familiar, and when the light was lowered from my eyes I turned my head to see who belonged to it, and Wally Sternaman stepped forward.

"You can lower your hands now, Matt," he said. "You look silly standing there like that. Fred, this is the kid from the *Chronicle* I was telling you about, Matt Althaus. Matt, meet Fred Thede."

I gave Wally's friend a trembling handshake, then jammed both hands into the pockets of my Levi's.

"Sorry if I scared you, Matt," said Fred, "but I thought we had us something here." Fred Thede was older, fifty maybe, and he was built like a wrestler with a face to match the build. Both of them were in border-patrol uniforms that were a little deeper than the color of army fatigues, and they wore what looked like government-issue fatigue caps.

"What in hell are you doing out here?" Wally asked. "When I told you on the phone I'd see you around, I didn't expect it to be this soon or under these circumstances."

"Well, I sure as anything didn't expect to meet you guys out here, either," I said. "Believe me, I didn't plan it this way."

"Wally here says you work for the paper," said Thede. "You looking for a story, or something?"

"I'm just curious."

"You watch it, sonny," said the older man. "You know what curiosity did to the rabbit."

"The cat, Freddie," said Wally. "It was the cat that curiosity killed."

"Well, it probably killed lots of rabbits, too, so, kid, you better watch what you get into."

"You can't blame a guy for being curious," I snapped at him. "There's no law against it."

"Come off it," Wally said. "Don't get your back up. 'Course there's no law against being curious, but we think we're making some progress on this case and— well, Matt, we just don't want anyone getting in our way and maybe getting hurt."

"What he means is, you start snooping in the wrong places and you'll blow it for us," said Fred Thede. "When the time comes we start moving, anyone in the way— he's just liable to get hurt."

"Promise me you'll forget about whatever it is you're up to," Wally said.

"I'm not promising anything," I said. I could feel my cheeks flushing with anger.

"Listen, sonny, this ain't fun and games," Thede said.

"We've got our job to do and it ain't an easy one, take it from me. We got a war going on here along the border, and every day we lose a little more ground. Ain't no way we're going to win this war, but we're sure as hell fighting our damnedest. You get in the way, you'll maybe lose this particular battle for us."

"You guys are just trying to scare me off." I'd heard just about enough.

"Don't put it that way," argued Wally. "We're not trying to scare anybody; we're trying to protect you. This is for real, and we don't want to see you or anybody else hurt."

"I'm not planning on getting hurt, Wally, and besides, I'm big enough to take care of myself. You guys just get off my back. Believe me, I'm not going to do anything to screw up your case."

"Just be careful, sonny," Thede said, poking a finger toward me, "and remember that rabbit."

Wally sighed. "The *cat*, Freddie, the *cat!*"

"Cat, rabbit, what the hell, that don't matter, anyway. Just so the kid understands." He looked at me, expecting an answer. I just shrugged and half nodded.

"Well, it's a cinch we can't do any good out here tonight," said Wally, looking at his watch. "Not after all this ruckus." Then he turned to me and asked if I wanted a lift into town.

I was tempted. I thought of the long ride home on that no-speed bike and I almost told him yes, but I had my pride to think of. "No thanks, Wally," I said. "I got wheels." I felt like kicking myself, but it was a matter of principle.

So Wally raised his hand in a wave and turned with Fred Thede and they walked over a ridge and disappeared. In a minute or two I heard an engine start, some gears shifting, and then the sound slowly disappeared.

It was another twenty minutes or more before I could find the bike in all that underbrush, and it was long after midnight when at last I chained the green monster to the light post next to the Railroad Hotel and climbed the steps to my room.

I guess it was because I was so tired and dragged out the next day, and wasn't at all what you could call sharp, that I messed up the way I did. At least I'll blame it on that because I have to blame it on something.

To begin with, that morning was a chaotic one, although that's no excuse. For some reason more news was happening that day in the world, the United States, Arizona, Papago County, and Crandall than on any other day since I'd been working on the *Chronicle*. Or maybe it just seemed that way.

Besides everything else happening in the world, a Crandall girl had been crowned Miss Papago County during the pageant in Corinth the night before and would be competing in the Miss Arizona contest; the local police had arrested a prominent business executive on charges of embezzling; the county's oldest resident, Miss Hattie Blakely, had celebrated her one-hundred-third birthday; there had been a rash of burglaries in Crandall the night before; and arson was suspected in a fire that destroyed a small grocery store in the poor part of town down near the border.

It was a lucky thing Mitch was on the desk, because if

it had been up to me to put it all together, I'd have blown it for sure. As it was, I blew it pretty well, anyway.

Bran spent the morning at his desk with his telephone pushed against his ear getting stories by telephone and banging them out in that rat-tat-tat machine-gun typing of his. The early part of the morning I spent at the police station getting details on the burglary rampage, the embezzling arrest and the other more routine police news. Then I went next door to the fire department and talked with the chief and got all the information from him about the grocery-store fire. From there I went over to Charlie Prentiss's photo studio and picked up a batch of photos he had for us. He had been driving home from Corinth the night before and heard the fire sirens, so he had a picture of the fire for that day's paper.

From his files he got a mug shot of the businessman who had been arrested, and he had a photo of Miss Hattie Blakely blowing out the candles on her birthday cake, and another one of the Crandall girl who had just been crowned Miss Papago County. I was happy we had plenty of pictures to go with our stories, because pictures really liven up the newspaper pages.

From the camera store I rode the bike back to the office and Bran turned on the machine and began making plastic engravings of all the pictures. Then I sat at my desk, arranged the notes, put a piece of copy paper in my typewriter and got to work. Fast as I'd finish a story, I'd pass it on to Mitch, who would edit it, write a headline and then send it down the chute to the back shop.

He was also handling the bumper crop of copy from Bran, as well as the wire stories from the Associated

Press machine, and everything else that came to his desk to be used. Mitch was working against a special deadline that morning on top of everything else, because the congressman who represented our district was in town and Mitch was having lunch with him at the Crandall House. Mitch planned to hurry home once the last of the copy had gone down to the shop, grab a quick shower and put on a coat and tie. When you go to lunch with a congressman, you don't want to be all grubby from a morning spent in a dirty newspaper office.

By eleven Bran had finished writing and left the newsroom to get together with some cotton farmers who were having a meeting in town, and about ten minutes after that, Mitch left for home and the shower. That left me in charge. All I had to do was catch the phones, work on a feature story about an old cowboy character I had interviewed, and, when all the engravings were finished, mark the right page number on the back of each with a red grease pencil, and take them down to the shop and get them cemented in the proper spaces that the printers had left for them in the big page forms. When the paper came off the press then, I had to check it over for any major errors.

I was having trouble with the lead paragraph of my cowboy feature; I just couldn't seem to get the right words down on paper. My mind kept drifting off to what had happened the night before with Wally Sternaman and his border-patrol partner, and to alien smuggling, and I tried to think of what I could do next in my investigation. It seemed as though I was at a dead end. There wasn't any place for me to go next. Yawning, I stood and stretched and went back to the bathroom and splashed cold water on my face, but that didn't help much. The muscles in my legs were so sore from all my bicycling the night before that they felt as though they were ready to fall off. After a while the last engraving was done and I marked the page numbers on all of them and took them downstairs and watched as a printer got them onto the page forms.

Shannon was at her desk so I stopped and talked with her for a while. Her friends were having a softball game at the city park that evening and we had been invited to play. If there was anything I felt like not doing that night, it was playing ball. I started ticking off all the reasons why I didn't want to play. When I was on reason number eleven the press started, and by reason sixteen a newsroom phone started ringing. I told her we'd finish the discussion later, then ran up the steps and grabbed the phone before it stopped ringing.

It was some drunk on the line phoning from one of the bars on Copper Avenue—I could hear the jukebox music in the background—and he wanted to know how many rounds the heavyweight championship bout went, when John L. Sullivan beat Jake somebody. "We got us one hell of an argument going here," the drunk said. "My pal here, he's trying to tell me the fight went more'n seventy rounds and I say it didn't go over twenty. Got five bucks riding on it—see if you can look it up for us."

That's one of the things you have to put up with in a newspaper office. People call all the time wanting to know weird things, and usually it's to settle some argument in a bar. They think newspaper people know everything, or at least know where to find out. I put the call on "hold" and thumbed through *The World Almanac*. Just then another phone rang. It was Mrs. Beckman, our correspondent up in Corinth, calling in a story about the county board of supervisors meeting. I told her to hang on a second, put *her* on "hold," then got back to the boxing fan at the tavern.

"Looks like you're out five bucks," I told him. "According to the almanac, John L. Sullivan beat Jake Kilrain on July 8, 1889, in Richburg, Mississippi. It was the last championship bare-knuckles bout, it says here, and it went seventy-five rounds."

"Seventy-five! That's gotta be wrong. Ain't no fight ever went seventy-five rounds!"

"Sorry, sir, but that's what it says here. I have to hang up now because I have a call on another line."

Then I was back with Mrs. Beckman again, and I put a fresh sheet of copy paper in my typewriter and told her to go ahead. As she dictated, I typed. While I was pecking away, Raul, from the back shop, came up and dropped a stack of fresh *Chronicles* on the big table and I nodded my thanks to him. The supervisors' story wasn't all that long, but Mrs. Beckman kept changing her mind about how she wanted to say things, and besides, I'm not the world's fastest typist. Finally we got to the end of her story and I was halfway across the newsroom on my way to check the day's paper, when the phone rang again.

It was Mrs. Fitzhugh. Was Trevor in? I told her he wasn't and she asked if he'd be in later that afternoon and I said probably not, and she sounded awfully unhappy when she hung up. At last things quieted down enough for me to check the paper for errors. The pile of them Raul had brought had been on the table for better than twenty minutes, and I hoped I wouldn't find anything wrong, because in twenty minutes a lot of papers can roll off the press, old and slow as it is.

When I saw what had happened I just couldn't believe it. I had made one of the worst possible mistakes. Some of the pictures and their captions, or cutlines, had somehow gotten switched.

All at once I felt weak and my heart started pounding and all I wanted to do was crawl into the bottom drawer of my desk and hide. Or die. Of course I knew I couldn't do that. The press had to be stopped, but fast.

Running down the stairs I almost knocked into Bran and Mitch, who had just come in, Bran after his meeting and Mitch before lunch.

"The pictures!" I hollered at them as we passed on the stairs, but I didn't pause to explain. I ran through the business office into the shop and all the way back to the press area.

"Stop it!" I hollered at Harvey, the shop foreman, trying to be heard above the noise of the press. "Stop it—stop the *press!*" I waved frantically at the press and ran my finger across my throat, hoping he'd understand. He nodded and hurried to the control panel, punched a button and slowly the press rumbled to a halt.

I looked out the back door and Jess Perry's truck was gone; that meant almost a thousand *Chronicles* were on their way to Corinth.

I was too late!

17

I DIDN'T EVEN have to explain to Mitch and Bran what had gone wrong. By the time I got back up to the newsroom both were holding newspapers and they already knew.

Under the photograph of sweet old Miss Hattie Blakely the cutline said:

Jailed for Embezzlement

Police officers today arrested 47-year-old Charles A. Barrington, longtime Crandall insurance executive, on charges of embezzling more than $36,000 from the company for which he works.

Details of the incident were in a story right below the photograph. On another page was the picture of the smiling high school girl who had been crowned Miss Papago County, and the caption beneath it read:

Still Spry at 103

Crandall's oldest resident, Miss Hattie Blakely, who came to Papago County in 1887 in a covered wagon, blows out the candles on her birthday cake during a party in her honor yesterday. Miss Blakely, who is 103 years young, remains active in the women's circle of the United Methodist Church.

And of course on another page was the photograph of the businessman—fat, bald and wearing a phony smile—who had been arrested. Under that picture it said:

Beauty Crowned

Dimpled Charlene Avis, 17, who will be a senior at Crandall High School in September, was chosen Miss Papago County during a pageant in Corinth last night. The petite, raven-haired beauty, head twirler with the Crandall Coyote Marching Band, twirled a pair of flaming batons in the talent portion of the competition. The daughter of Mr. and Mrs. Conn Avis, Charlene is looking forward to a modeling career in Los Angeles after graduation.

It just couldn't have been worse. Maybe some day we'd all be able to laugh about it, but at that moment there was nothing funny about the situation. Bran and Mitch both were on their feet.

"How many papers are we talking about?" Bran asked Mitch.

"I'd say probably twelve, maybe fourteen hundred," answered Mitch. "Harvey'll know for sure."

"And most of 'em in Jess's truck headed for Corinth?" Bran asked, and Mitch nodded. Bran reached into his pocket for his car keys and tossed them to me. "Why doesn't Mark take my car and try to catch up with Jess?" suggested Bran. I was all set to make for the stairs. Mitch frowned though, and shook his head.

"Think I'd better go after Jess," Mitch said, biting his lip.

"But you've got the lunch with the congressman," I said.

"That'll keep," Mitch said. "We're facing potential lawsuits here—this is an emergency. I'll have Shannon go over to the Crandall House and have lunch with the congressman. They're old friends. She's known him all her life." Then Mitch turned to me.

"Matt, you hop on that bike of yours and chase old Mr. Montaño. Hit all the stores and offices along Copper Avenue where he leaves papers—tell the people there was a mechanical problem and that the papers will be replaced. Yank 'em out of their hands if you have to. We'll have Harvey make the corrections right away and get the press running again soon as he can. And Bran, you take your Maverick and get down to the east side street corners where the circulation truck drops bundles for the carrier boys. Grab the bundles before those kids do. We've got to get back every single copy of the paper, if possible."

"You're sure you don't want me to go after Jess?" I asked. "After all, I feel like I'm to blame and I hate for you to miss your lunch with the congressman."

"That's all right, son—we all make mistakes. I just don't like the idea of your being in a racing situation on the highway. Besides, I know better where Jess will be heading in case he reaches Corinth before I catch him. You and Bran take care of the papers here in town and I imagine we'll be all set."

So I flipped Bran his keys and I ran down the steps

and took off. I really didn't care if I ever saw that bicycle again, but there I was, climbing aboard again, and rolling after Mr. Montaño. My legs still ached from the night before, but there was nothing else I could do. I was paying the price for goofing up. As I pedaled down the street I wondered why Mitch was so determined to go after Jess himself and have to miss that lunch with the congressman, or at least be late for it, but I guessed he just wanted to be sure he got all the copies of the *Chronicle* that were bound for Corinth.

That afternoon was a nightmare, but between the three of us we managed to find just about every copy of the paper that had come off the press with the switched pictures in them. When we sat in the office talking about it later, Mitch said he didn't suppose that the few papers that we might have missed would cause any legal problems for us. At least he hoped they wouldn't. I hoped so, too.

All that had happened Friday and it was the worst Friday of my life. About the only thing good about that day was that it was followed by Saturday and Sunday, which just happened to be the greatest weekend of my life.

On Saturday morning we put out the paper that carried the Sunday date and colored comics, and that was a breeze. It was mostly features and AP wire news, because the government offices were closed on Saturday morning, except of course, for the police and fire departments, which never closed. We had that edition wrapped up in no time.

All morning I kept expecting Mitch to light into me at

any second and chew me out for the stupid picture switch I had pulled on Friday, but that didn't happen. Chewing out is not Mitch's way. When the paper had come off the press and we had checked it for errors, Mitch, Shan and I walked over to the drugstore and had a sandwich. Mitch bought. Not once did he bring up the subject of my big screw-up.

We were perched on stools at the counter with Shan between us, just jabbering about one thing and another.

"Got any great plans for the weekend?" he asked me.

"We're going to the dance tonight," Shan put in before I could answer Mitch. She wasn't going to let me forget that. The country club was having its summer dance that evening for what the club bulletin called "the younger set," and for a couple of weeks Shan and I had talked about going.

Mitch asked if I had plans for that afternoon and I looked at Shan and she shook her head and so I told Mitch I was free.

"I've been wanting you to see the ranch," Mitch said then. "If you can squeeze it in, we could drive out early this afternoon and spend an hour or two on horseback. Of course I'd be sure to get you back in plenty of time for the dance."

I asked Shan if she was going out to the ranch, too, and she said she'd love to, but she had a million things she wanted to get done that afternoon. Seeing as how I had exactly zero things to do that afternoon, I accepted. I hadn't been horseback riding since I was about ten years old, but I figured I could handle it.

The closer we got to the ranch, the more Mitch seemed

to relax. Of course he was always cool and easygoing, but driving out to the place he seemed even more at ease than usual.

At the gate I hopped out of the car and pulled it open wide, then closed and latched it again after Mitch drove the station wagon through. We pulled up beside the corral. There were two horses in it, both saddled, both tied to the fence, and as we got out of the car, a man walked toward us from the bunkhouse. He was tall, with big shoulders, a not very pleasant face and a twitch in one eye. He wore a big hat, cowboy boots, Levi's that were clean and pressed, and a western shirt.

"Appreciate your saddling up for us," Mitch called to the cowboy as he approached us.

"Figured I might as well do it 'fore I got cleaned up. I'm fixin' to drive into town presently," and then he added, as if to explain, "Saturday."

"Matt, meet Larry Rylow—Larry looks after the place for us. Larry, Matt Althaus."

We shook hands and I told him I was happy to meet him and he mumbled something back to me. Up close he smelled, but not the way you'd expect a cowboy to smell. Mitch noticed it, too.

"You smell awfully good, Larry," Mitch told him.

The cowboy looked embarrassed and toed the ground with his pointed boot. "Some fancy-smellin' new stickum I'm tryin' on my hair," he said. "Lilac, something. Hope it holds as powerful as it smells."

"Don't bother waiting for us, Larry," said Mitch. "We'll unsaddle and turn the horses loose in the corral when we're done. You go ahead into town, but watch out for those pretty girls, smelling as good as you do."

Larry smiled a crooked smile, told Mitch he was obliged, touched his fingertips to his hat brim and walked back to the bunkhouse.

"Larry doesn't have a whole lot to say," Mitch told me as he opened the corral gate, "but he's dependable. Takes good care of the place and that keeps my mind at ease."

Being a city boy, I know a little less than nothing about horses, so I'll just say Mitch's horse was a deep brown with white markings on its head and one foot, and mine was a dirty-looking gray. Mitch said the gray was old enough not to be skitterish, but young enough to have some spirit. I hoped it didn't have *too* much spirit. Mitch tightened the cinches, then stood by while I mounted. My stirrups didn't need adjusting, so then he mounted and I followed him out of the corral.

We passed the big new barn and Mitch looked over at it like it was his most valued possession, then he reined his horse away from the scatter of buildings and out into the desert. We climbed steadily. Now and again Mitch would rein up and wait for me to ride up beside him and he would explain something to me or point out a landmark and a few times he just wanted to ask how I was getting along. It was an easy ride and my horse was as surefooted and steady as Mitch had promised. Already though, I could feel my thighs beginning to ache, but I had expected that, so I didn't complain. I'd just suffer in silence. He sat easy and looked as though he belonged on that horse, almost like he was a part of it. Mitch looked lots more comfortable in the saddle than he did in the editor's chair, and much more natural.

It was beautiful country we rode through, with lacy paloverde trees and mesquites and clumps of desert grasses and bushes here and there, and lots of cactus. The Arizona desert was much greener and more covered with growing things than I had imagined it would be. It took a while to get used to it, having lived in the Midwest all my life, but I was beginning to like it. For a while we followed an arroyo, then Mitch led the way to the top of a hill and we dismounted there.

Holding the reins with one hand, Mitch pointed with the other, off into the distance. "That far hill," he said, "that's our property line. Beyond it is some grazing land we're going to be leasing from the government." Turning to the opposite direction, he pointed toward a distant stand of tall cottonwoods. Those trees followed the course of an underground river, he explained, and it marked the ranch's boundary in that direction. "And back behind us we're bounded by the highway, and"— pointing again—"by an imaginary line that runs through the mountains over in that direction."

For a while he stood beside the horse, gazing off at the acres of ranchland. "It'll be a small operation," he said, almost as if to himself, "but it'll keep us busy, and one of these days it'll be paying for itself." Those few minutes we stood there gave me a preview of just how sore my legs were going to be. They really began to ache. We remounted and I followed Mitch into a small canyon and we threaded upward, through it.

The canyon was as beautiful as anything I'd ever seen.

It was narrow at the mouth and then it widened, and far ahead I could see that it narrowed again, with the trail disappearing between two walls of sheer, red rock that rose hundreds of feet. Small animals scampered about and there were birds in the air. The trail followed a small stream that was clear as glass, and bubbled toward the valley below and probably disappeared somewhere way off, into the dry desert sands. It was all so quiet and peaceful that I didn't once think about anything else, not even my big alien smuggling story.

Riding slowly, Mitch turned his head my way and said that up far ahead in the higher country was a mountain meadow where his cattle would graze—when he got some cattle—during the hot summer months. He said we wouldn't have time to ride all the way up there and I was relieved, because I knew my legs couldn't take that much more. I was really suffering. Finally we stopped again on a flat point that looked out over the valley below. Far in the distance I could see the cluster of buildings that was the headquarters of the Garrity ranch, and I shuddered at the thought of riding all the way back there. I tried not to think about that though, because the view was a beautiful one and I wanted to enjoy it.

"You really love this country, don't you, Mitch?"

"Does it show that much?" he answered, breaking into a smile. "I thought I had a better poker face than that."

We sat on our horses looking out over the valley and not saying anything for a couple of minutes, and finally Mitch broke the silence.

"Yes," he said, "this is the place for me. I'm afraid I've about had my fill of newspapering, Matt. I've found something I like better—a lot better."

I almost fell off the horse when I heard that. I had grown up thinking my Uncle Mitch loved newspaper work more than anything else in the world, except for Aunt Beth and Shannon, of course.

"You look surprised, Matt."

"I am. I mean, I had no idea. Are you planning to quit the *Chronicle* and move out here?"

"That's right," he said. "Oh, not soon—not as soon as I'd like. I'd do it tomorrow if I could, but there's a little matter of money." He paused and sat with one leg crossed over the saddle in front of him, resting, sort of dreaming, gazing off into the distance. "But one of these days, Matt, one of these days."

"But I always thought you loved being a newspaper-man."

"There was a time when I did, but I'm afraid it's past. I think the business has just gotten to me. Wears a man down sometimes, and I've had my fill of it, as I said. I've had enough of fighting deadlines and sitting through boring school-board meetings that go on far into the night, and I've had enough of writing social items about somebody's Aunt Eleanor visiting here for three days, and I've had enough of writing sob stories about people who are sick and poor and have nowhere to turn, and I've had enough of writing about people who are in trouble with the law."

Mitch stopped talking and looked over at me. "I'm sorry, son. I didn't mean to go on like that. I suppose what I'm trying to say—and not doing very well—is that I've had it up to my eyeballs. I'm ready for this place, ready for the wide open spaces, as they say in the Westerns. At heart I'm a rancher, I suppose—a cowboy—and not a newsman."

It was hard for me to understand why anyone would ever want to get out of the newspaper business. As far as I was concerned, there wasn't any kind of work a person could do in the whole world that would be better than being a newspaperman. I told Mitch how I felt.

"Maybe I was never cut out for it in the first place," he said. "I went back to college after Korea—didn't have the slightest idea of what I wanted to do—and I took a couple of classes in the journ school. They were easy for me and—well, before I knew it I had a degree in journalism and a job on a newspaper. It just happened, Matt. I didn't plan it. Now, you take Bran—he's a real newsman. Always was, always will be."

"It's funny, Mitch—funny peculiar, I mean, not funny ha-ha—your wanting out of the business so you can ranch, and Bran's not being able to stay away from it, even after he's retired."

Mitch chuckled and said he hoped I wasn't disappointed in him. "Oh, no," I said, "I could never be disappointed in *you*. And the way you put it—about wanting to have your own place like this—it makes sense, really. Like my social studies teacher last year kept saying, this world would be in one big mess if everybody wanted to do the same kind of work."

"Your teacher has a head on his shoulders," Mitch said, and then he glanced at his watch.

"Think we'd better ride on back," he said. "If you don't mind the company of golden-agers, Beth and I thought we'd take you and Shannie to dinner at the club tonight before the dance. 'Course, after dinner we'll head home and leave you youngsters alone."

I told Mitch that would be great and then I realized what I had said. "I don't mean it would be great for you to leave us alone—I mean it would be great to go to dinner with you."

He laughed and turned his horse and clucked it into motion, and my old gray followed. We didn't stop or talk all the way back to the corral, so I did plenty of thinking about what Mitch had told me about his leaving the newspaper business and I couldn't help but feel sorry about it, yet I could understand.

If a person isn't happy in his work and he has a chance to switch to something he likes better, more power to him. I knew I'd be awfully unhappy if I had to work in a bank or in an insurance office all day when what I really wanted was to be a reporter.

Still, I felt sad about Mitch.

18

WHAT MITCH HAD said about leaving the newspaper business bothered me, and I tried not to think about it. Sore and aching as I was, I enjoyed the ride with him. Just being with Mitch was something special. When I was with him it wasn't at all like being with a grown-up. I didn't have to be careful of what I said or did because I knew that Mitch understood me. I felt comfortable with him, if you know what I mean. And I guessed I'd think as much of him when he was a rancher as I always had. Driving back to town we joked and laughed a lot, and when he dropped me off at the hotel he told me Shan would pick me up for dinner about seven o'clock.

It was the first time all summer that I'd worn a coat and tie, and it wasn't very comfortable, but when I saw how great Shan looked I forgot all about being uncomfortable. Shan and I drove directly to the club and met Beth and Mitch there. They had driven in their other car. There was no doubt about it, Aunt Beth and Shan were the most beautiful women in the dining room. I hadn't seen Beth really dressed up since I was small, and she looked fantastic, for an older woman. Beautiful. But I had trouble keeping my eyes off Shannon.

She couldn't have looked greater. Her hair and makeup and clothes all looked just perfect. Shan might've been a model for shampoo or toothpaste in an ad in one of those girls' magazines.

Her three-colors-of-blonde hair was piled on top of her head and it was loose, and sort of tumbling, and for the first time that summer she was wearing eye shadow and a touch of lipstick. Her dress was from Mexico; it was long, and just a shade darker than white, and it was cut low in front and the whole top of it was covered with tiny flowers of every color that she said were hand-embroidered.

When we were finished eating, Mitch and Beth told us good night and we went into the banquet room, which was set up for the dance, and they stayed at the table in the dining room to have a brandy before going home early. The group that played for the dance had come down from Corinth, and they weren't really sensational, but they played some pretty decent music. My legs were killing me, really killing me, but I didn't want to let on that they were and spoil the evening. As far as I was concerned I wanted to dance every dance with Shan. If I had to suffer, I'd suffer the next morning.

Shan knew everybody there. I saw some of my snipe-hunting friends, and Shan introduced me to a lot of kids I hadn't met before. There were quite a few older ones home from college for the summer and the banquet room was crowded. The only thing wrong with the whole evening was that it slipped by too fast. As far as I was concerned, it could have lasted all night. It didn't, though. At midnight the group played its last number and the lights were turned up bright.

Some of the kids were going for pizza afterward and Shan asked if I felt like going with them. I wasn't hungry and I just shrugged. "Up to you," I said. "You want to go with them?"

"I'd rather just be with you, Matt." I didn't argue.

Shan handed me the car keys and I drove the wagon. We stopped first at a drive-in and bought a couple of Cokes in king-sized paper cups, and when I settled back in the car I asked her where she wanted to go.

"The Hill," she said, and she gave directions as I drove. It turned out to be a small mountain—at least that's what we would call it back in the Midwest—that was a mile or so north of town. A road wound its way up the mountain to the top, which was fairly flat and had enough room for several cars to park. The view took in both Crandall and La Pizca, and it surprised me how many lights there were and how large the two cities looked when you viewed them together from that height. We weren't alone up there.

We saw a couple of cars filled with kids who had been at the dance, and we saw several other kids who hadn't. We got out of the wagon and walked to the edge of the parking area for a better view and Shan pointed out different places. I could see the big neon sign that was on top of the Crandall House (the "u" on the sign was burned out and it said "Crandall Hose"), and using that for bearings I could figure out just about where the *Chronicle* office was. Shan showed me where she lived and then she pointed out the Railroad Hotel. At least where we would've seen it if there had been any lights showing. All the old people in the hotel had probably been asleep for hours.

After a while we settled down on a low rock wall and finished our Cokes, and then dropped the cups into a big litter can as we wandered back toward the wagon. We stopped to talk with some people Shan knew and then got into our car. I slipped my arm around Shan and she curled up closer. At a time like that I always have trouble thinking of something romantic to say, so I just kissed her. Kissing beats talking any day. But then suddenly she drew away from me.

"What's wrong?" I asked.

"I'm worried about you, Winky. I keep thinking about all the awful things you could be getting into with your investigating thing. I don't want you to get hurt."

"To be honest, I think that's about over," I told her. "I don't know what to do next and I'm just not getting anywhere. Unless I get a bright idea pretty quick, my great story won't ever get written."

"Then why don't you forget it, Matt? You only have a few more weeks here and I hate to think of your spending all that time out—well, out doing whatever it is you've been doing. Maybe I'm selfish, but there's so little time, I'd rather we spent it together." Shan reached up and ran her long fingernails through my hair, then pulled my head down and kissed me.

"You trying to bribe me?"

"If that's what you want to call it." Her voice had a pout in it.

"Okay, I'll make a deal. If I don't get onto something in a day or two I'll give up and forget it. Sound fair?"

"But what if you *do* get onto something?" she asked. "Then what?"

"Then I'll just have to follow through and see what happens. Okay?"

She didn't like that idea.

"Just a couple of days, Shan." I almost felt like I was begging her.

"Okay, Winky," she said, brightening. "But promise me you'll forget that stupid business then."

I promised her and then I kissed her to show I meant it. We were still kissing when my right leg went ape. It was almost like somebody had jammed a dagger into the muscle on the inside of my thigh. I went straight up and my head bumped the ceiling of the car.

"What's wrong?" Shan sounded frightened.

"My leg," I yelped, and then I repeated, "my *leg!*"

I yanked the handle on the door and jumped outside and stomped around. Shannon came right out after me. "But what *is* it with your leg?" she wanted to know. I started hopping up and down on the dumb leg and at the same time working at that muscle with the fingers of both hands.

"Charley horse or something," I said through clenched teeth. She put an arm around my shoulder and tried to keep me from falling down. "Only it's worse than any charley horse I ever had in my life." People from other cars came over to see what the commotion was.

Everybody wanted to know what was wrong and whether we needed some help. All I needed was to be left alone. One wise guy asked Shan what she had done to me and if I hadn't been hurting so much I'd have slugged him. All I could do was swear at him under my breath as I hopped. Shan told them I had a leg cramp and that everything was all right and they went back to their cars.

Finally the sharp pain went away, but it still ached in that muscle. "I better get you home," Shannon said. "What do you think caused it?"

She held my arm to steady me as I limped around the car to the passenger side and then she opened the door and I got in carefully. She went around to the other side and slid in behind the steering wheel.

"I guess I've expected too much of my legs the last few days," I said after she got the car started. I told her about my long bike ride two nights before and reminded her that her dad and I had ridden for better than three hours that afternoon and that I hadn't been on a horse for almost half my life.

"And then tonight, I don't think we missed a dance," I went on as she found the road that led to the bottom of the Hill. "But what really touched it off though, was just now, sitting here in the car. I had my right leg bent and pulled up so I could sort of face you and—aw, forget it, Shan." I realized how stupid I must've sounded trying to explain all that.

She laughed. "I'm sorry, Matt, I really am. I don't mean to laugh because I know you were really in pain, but your story sounds so . . . so . . ."

"*Stupid!*" I said. "That's the word for it, *stupid!*"

"Not stupid, but funny. Sad-funny, though. I'm sorry I laughed, but I couldn't help it." She let her hand rest on my leg as she drove and before I knew it I began to laugh, too. I guess it was pretty funny after all, even if my thigh didn't see the humor in it.

Shan drove up in front of the hotel and turned off the lights but left the engine running.

"Why don't we swim tomorrow before dinner? That'll work some of the soreness out of your legs."

"Will you pick me up?" I asked. "I'd hate to have to pedal the green monster all the way out to your place, the way I'm feeling."

"I'll be here at two."

Then Shan reached over and pulled me close to her and patted my back, the way my mother used to when I was small and had hurt myself.

"My poor, poor Winky," she said, and she kissed me, then pushed me toward the door. "You take it upstairs and put it to bed. The sleep should help."

It was all I could do to climb out of the car. I was hurting from my waist down and didn't feel all that great from my waist up, either. What a way to end what had started out as a great evening. Sometimes I'm such a clod!

I told her good night and shut the door and began walking toward the hotel steps. "Winky," she called, and I stopped and went back to the car. Leaning over, I looked at her through the open window.

"Yeah?" I said without much enthusiasm.

"Winky," Shannon said, "sometimes you're awfully

funny, but I love you." Flipping on the car lights, she drove off.

A sort of chill went through my body as I stood there, but it was a warm chill, if there can be such a thing. Already my legs felt better as I limped toward the steps again.

19

BETH LAUGHED SO hard Sunday evening that she got the hiccups. It's a wonder I didn't, because I laughed even harder than she did.

When I made myself get out of bed that morning, I was stiffer than I had expected to be, but not as sore. I ate breakfast in the hotel dining room and then did my laundry and while it was in the washing machine, I wrote a letter home. In my letters I tried to tell my folks everything—well, almost everything—I'd been doing, and that way I'd have a sort of diary of my summer. By the time the letter and laundry were finished, it was time for me to get ready to go swimming.

Right at two o'clock Shan picked me up and we stopped at a drive-in for some burgers and fries and Cokes and ate as we drove out to the club. The pool was crowded, the way it always was on Sundays. Going to the country club for a swim on Sunday afternoons was one of the big social highlights of the week in Crandall. We found a place almost to ourselves in the grass near the wall, and spread our beach towels there and settled down. I swam a lot during the afternoon and tried to use my legs more than I usually do when I swim, hoping that all the kicking would work some of the soreness out, and it did. We soaked up plenty of rays, too, and I think the heat helped.

By the time we got to the Garritys' house my legs were feeling lots better. Bran was there for dinner, too, and Beth had fixed Mexican food. Her tacos were the best I had ever eaten anywhere, and she had made chilis relleños and bean tostadas and Mexican cornbread. During that summer I had developed a taste for Mexican food and I hated to think of going back home where Mexican food wasn't as popular or very good.

After dinner Mitch and Bran and I cleaned up the kitchen while Beth and Shan sat on stools at the breakfast bar and supervised and cracked jokes. Afterward we all went out into the patio and sat in lawn chairs, just taking it easy. It was dark now and it was cool and pleasant on the patio. We played a word game for a while, but mostly we just talked.

Conversation got around to the *Chronicle* and of course the matter of my famous three-way picture switch got considerable mention. "We're all just lucky that we got most of the papers back," Mitch said. "They really could have nailed us for that—three ways!"

Bran said he had to admit that it was one of the better picture switches he had come across in all of his years in the newspaper business. In fact, he said, it was the first triple switch he'd ever heard about. Usually it's just a two-way switch.

"Two can be bad enough," Mitch said.

"That's Matt for you," Shannon teased. "Whenever he does something, he does it well."

"You can be sure that I have a copy of it in my collection of typographical errors and misprints," Bran said.

Beth told him she imagined his collection would make marvelous reading and Bran told her she was right.

"Now and again I'll come across it and flip through the pages and it's always good for a laugh or two," Bran said. "But Mark's contribution will have a special spot in the collection." He looked at me and grinned, as if he thought I should be proud of myself for goofing up.

"I remember hearing of one classic switch," said Mitch, "but for the life of me I can't remember what newspaper it was. Doesn't matter—it involved photos of a girl scout who had been honored for some achievement or other, and a desperate sex fiend who had been arrested for a long string of terrible crimes. You can imagine the stir *that* one caused."

All evening Beth had been in a laughing mood and she began to chuckle then, and seemed to be having trouble stopping. But Bran had a tale to tell and that did it.

"There's one I heard about years ago, although I never saw it in print myself. A major daily—Chicago, I think—carried two pics on the front page one day. The first one was of a very socially prominent elderly woman, who had died the day before, and the other was of an ugly old warehouse that had been destroyed by fire.

"Under the photo of the burning warehouse the display line said, 'Will Be Missed by Chicago Society,' which wasn't really too bad, but the line under the old woman's picture said, 'Old Eyesore Gone at Last.'"

That's when Beth got the hiccups. Bran's story must've really struck her funny. The rest of us were laughing hard, too. Shan went to the kitchen and got her mother a glass of water and that helped some, but not much. She hiccupped the rest of the evening.

We talked for a while more—Beth wanted to know what news I'd had from my parents and so I filled her in—and then Mitch asked me if I'd recuperated from the horseback ride.

I grimaced and told him I was still hurting, but not as much.

"How long did he keep you out there?" Beth asked.

"Oh, two, three hours," I said. "I really enjoyed it, though. That's such a great place you have out there. That scenery is unbelievable."

"Yes, but Mitchell should have known better than to keep you on a horse so long, your not being used to riding," Beth said.

"I didn't mind it," I said. "And it wasn't until the end of the ride that I began hurting. Besides, I liked hearing about your plans to move out there and work the ranch."

Looking at her husband she said, "Mitch, I just hope you didn't bore poor Matt to death with all that ranch talk." Every few words she spoke were underlined with a hiccup.

Mitch grinned at me and shrugged, and slid lower in his chair.

"I suppose I should have warned you, Matt," Beth said. "When Mitch pulls on his boots and puts that

Stetson on his head, why, something comes over him, like a spell of some kind. There's just no stopping him then. Talk, talk, talk—and all about horses and cattle. *Hon*estly." She looked at Mitch again with a wrinkled-nose expression and reached over to squeeze his hand. "You're just lucky he got you back in time for the dance."

There was some more laughing and then a pause in the conversation. Somebody yawned and before you knew it, all of us were yawning. Yawns are almost as catching as laughter and chicken pox.

"I hate to be the one to break up this fine gathering," Bran said, "but *I* have to work tomorrow." Then he leaned over toward me and said in a loud, stage whisper, "Truth is, about this time of night Mitch gets out his guitar and starts singing songs from his college days."

"Oh, I'd like to hear him sing," I said.

"No, you wouldn't, kid," Bran said. "Take it from me, you wouldn't."

"Just for that," said Mitch, "I'll let you work desk tomorrow."

"That's the thanks I get for trying to save an innocent young man some pain and suffering," Bran said, standing up. Then he looked at me. "Want a ride home, Mark?"

Before I could answer Shannon told him that it would be out of the way for him to drive me, and besides, it was bad luck for a dinner guest to arrive in one car and leave in another.

Bran said that was one superstition he hadn't heard before.

"I know," said Shan. "I just made it up." By that time we were all punchy, like there was an epidemic of ha-ha

going around, and we were all laughing again. After
thanking Beth, Bran left the patio and it wasn't many
minutes before Shan and I left, too.

Driving back to the hotel I scrunched down, put my
head back and closed my eyes. I was beat, yet I was wide
awake, as though I could keep going all night. I was
really hyped up. Sometimes you get that way.

"Your folks are the greatest," I said to Shan.

"So you noticed, too."

"I've always known it, especially about Mitch. I think
he's got to be one of the all-time cool people. I wish he'd
have played his guitar, though."

"No, you don't. Bran's right. Daddy's playing is
terrible and his voice is even worse. He doesn't remember half the words of those old college songs and he hums
where he doesn't know the words and—well, it's awful."

"How can you say such a thing about your own
father?"

"I've heard him."

After a minute or so of silence I told her I felt badly
about Mitch's wanting to leave the newspaper business.

"I guess he's just not made for the deadlines and all
the worry and bitchiness you have to take on a small-
town paper," Shan said. "Don't get me wrong—I think
he does a great job—but he really longs for the quiet life,
the ranch thing."

"But how about you? Do you want to live out in the
boonies like that?"

"I've never really thought about it, Matt. With Daddy,
I think a lot of it is just talk, wishful thinking. It's
probably a long way off, and besides, in another year I'll

be going away to college and just spending summers at home. It wouldn't be all that much different, anyway, because the ranch is only twenty minutes from town. It wouldn't be like we were living miles and miles from nowhere. Wherever Mom and Dad are happiest—that's fine with me."

Shan pulled up in front of the hotel and flipped off the headlights. I sat up and turned to face her, hoping that charley horse wouldn't come back again.

"It was a neat evening," I told her. "Are you as good a cook as your mom?"

"I'm learning. She's a good teacher."

"Some day you'll have to cook a dinner for me."

"Okay, but you'll have to do the dishes."

I thunked her on the back of her head with my knuckle and she jabbed a fingernail in my ribs. I grabbed her wrist to protect myself and suddenly she relaxed and I put my other arm around her and pulled her close and kissed her.

All at once the whole world was filled with lights that were flashing and blinking bright red and yellow and blue and I jerked away from Shan. I knew I liked her—loved her, I guess—but I didn't realize her kisses would have that much of an effect on me. The lights went out then, as quickly as they had begun, and I looked out the rear window.

It was a police car. What had we done? I wondered. Surely they couldn't arrest us for a little bit of innocent necking.

Or could they?

20

Tomas! Who but Tomas could it have been?

He was scrunched down behind the steering wheel, grinning like an idiot when I got out of Shan's car. Some joke.

"It's okay," I said to her. "It's just Tomas."

Climbing out of the patrol car, he walked over to the station wagon to tell Shan hello.

"What's the idea with all those lights?" I asked him. "You really put the fear in me."

"Just a little police humor," Tomas said. "You're just lucky I didn't use the siren."

"Did you want to talk to us or something?" I asked him.

"I'd rather talk with the lady," he said. "She's a lot prettier than you, Matt, but it's you I have to have a word with."

"Well, if that's supposed to be a hint, I get the message," said Shannon. She turned on the headlights, put the car in gear, then threw me a kiss and told us both good night. Tomas and I watched as the wagon rolled to the end of the block, then turned in the direction of the

Garrity home. We stepped to the police car and Tomas leaned against it and I sat up on the front fender. My legs were beginning to ache again.

"Haven't talked with you for a while, horse. How's it goin'?"

"I've been pretty busy."

"I think if I had a girl friend like Shannon, I'd be pretty busy, too."

"Then you know why I'd rather spend my evenings with her than riding around in a patrol car with you." Tomas said he could understand that. "And they've been keeping me pretty busy days at the paper, too," I added.

"You still liking it?"

"More than ever. This summer has been great for me. It's helped me make up my mind, and now I know for sure I want to go into journalism."

"That's good," said Tomas. "It helps if you like the work you're doing. Like me, I like being a cop."

"Is that why you waited around and flashed your lights? Just to tell me you like being a cop?"

"Well, that sort of brings it to the point, doesn't it? No, horse, it's just that I'm concerned about you. Saw Wally the other day and he was really ticked off at you for stumbling into their stakeout."

"Tough," I answered. "I feel the same way about them stumbling into *my* stakeout."

"Come off it, Matt. They were there as professionals—it's their job. You were just messing around and you could have been hurt."

"But I wasn't," I answered sarcastically.

"I'm happy for that, but what really upset Wally and

Fred Thede was that they found out later that while they were playing games with you, a big batch of illegals crossed not a mile away and were picked up by the smugglers a little later in the evening."

"After we'd all left the area?"

Tomas nodded.

"And they blame me because they didn't catch them?"

"In a way they do. Wally is a little bit unhappy about it, but Thede—he's *really* seeing red. Wally says he can understand what you're up to, but Fred is strictly business. He's all by the book and doesn't want any amateurs messing around."

"So why are you telling me all this, Tomas?"

"I guess I feel responsible in a way, because I brought you and Wally together. Wally unloaded on me last night over a beer. He said you'd make it a lot easier for all concerned if you'd stick with your typewriter and forget the detective stuff."

I swore under my breath. Nobody takes a kid reporter seriously—especially a kid *investigative* reporter. Woodward and Bernstein were young when they uncovered the Watergate business. I wondered if people took *them* seriously when they were working on their stories.

"Tomas, when you see Wally, you can tell him not to worry. I'll be going home before long, and as of right now I'm at a dead end, anyway. Unless I have some fantastic luck in the next couple of days, my alien smuggling story is dead."

The policeman asked if I was expecting any such fantastic run of luck and I laughed. "Not really," I said.

Tomas had a call over the police radio—a family

disturbance out in the east end of town—and he climbed into the car, picked up the microphone, and acknowledged the message. I dropped down off the fender and told Tomas good night. He raised his hand in a salute, then drove off.

That night I had trouble getting to sleep. I kept thinking about the great alien smuggling exposé I'd probably never get to write, and about Shan, and how I'd soon have to be leaving her. Sure, we'd be writing to each other as we had promised, but a bunch of letters wasn't quite like being together. By the time I finally did drop off to sleep I had about decided to forget the smuggling story and just spend as much time with Shan as I could during the rest of my days in Crandall. I realized she was the most important thing to me just then. I had never known a girl like her before—one who I found myself wanting to be with all the time. I'd be a fool if I blew it and didn't spend every possible second with her.

In the *Chronicle* office the next day I had my "fantastic stroke of luck," if you want to look at it that way.

As usual I stopped at the police station on my way in, and checked over the reports and scribbled my notes, then made for the office. Mitch was taking a story over the phone from our reporter in Corinth, and Bran was working desk. I had a lot to write, so got right to work. It was when I pulled open my drawer to get a pencil that I noticed it. It looked as though someone had gone through my things and disturbed the notes I had been putting together on the illegal aliens. But maybe it was just my imagination. It could have been that. I hoped so at least.

I couldn't be sure, but I had the feeling that the typed pages of notes weren't in the same order I had left them. Who could it have been?

A chill came over me. Bran? Could it have been Bran, the World War II correspondent I had idolized for so long? Then I remembered how the other day when I was typing the notes, he had seemed so curious, so interested in what I was doing. Had his curiosity gotten the better of him? I wondered. And he had warned me then to stay away from the illegal alien story.

Of course 'most everybody in Crandall had been warning me to do that. Wally Sternaman and Fred Thede had told me to keep out of it, and so had Tomas. And Shan—she hadn't really *warned* me not to get involved, but she had told me she worried about my getting hurt. Just about everybody I knew was either warning me or worrying about me. But Bran mixed up in the smuggling business? It couldn't be. Maybe he was just trying to scoop me on my own story.

But there wasn't time to sit and fret about it just then, though. I looked up at the clock. There was a lot to do before deadline time, so I started typing.

Later when Bran went down to the shop to check on the makeup, I asked Mitch how Bran usually spent his evenings.

"Why do you ask?" Mitch wanted to know.

"Just curious, I guess."

"To tell you the truth, I honestly don't know. Bran

is—well, he's a very private person. Doesn't talk a whole lot about himself. He putters around his place quite a bit—enjoys gardening—and I know he does a lot of reading. And he's working on a novel, too. Says it's the book he's been wanting to write for years. I don't have any idea what it's about, but I imagine we'll all know when the time is right."

Mitch asked if that satisfied my curiosity and I shrugged my shoulders and said I guessed it did, and I thanked him. He folded up some copy paper and stuck it in his pocket then and left the office to cover a chamber of commerce luncheon meeting. I had to cover one once and it was the dullest meeting I ever sat through. I almost fell asleep that time and was glad I didn't have to cover it that day. A few minutes later Bran came up the stairs into the newsroom.

"Got a problem, Mark," he said. "Nothing major, but a bother. Our banner story on page one—the income tax piece—runs about eight inches long and needs to be cut. I'll trim it, but I'd like you to go down and see that the boys in the shop lift the right grafs. I've got to stick close to the phone—long distance."

For a few minutes Bran worked on the copy with his pencil, then handed me the story. As I left the newsroom his phone was ringing. Good timing. All the page forms were already on the press except for the front page, and two of the boys were standing by waiting for the marked copy. I stood over them as they yanked the lines of type Bran had marked, then fit the rest of the type into the hole on page one. It fit perfectly.

Harvey the shop foreman and I looked over the page form and then he tightened the type in the frame and rolled it on the high wheeled table it rested on, over to the press. He slid the form from the table into the right position on the press and locked it in place. While he was making final adjustments, Jess Perry backed his big truck up to the loading dock.

One of the shop men called out to him that the truck was over too much to one side. "You gonna have trouble opening the rear door," he hollered. Jess climbed down from the cab to have a look for himself.

Hands on hips, he stood briefly studying the situation, then grumbled to himself as he climbed back into the cab. He started the engine and shifted from reverse into low. At least he tried to. The gears ground in a loud, grating noise that was enough to set your teeth on edge, then almost whined, as they fell into place. Everybody in the shop laughed.

"Grind *me* a pound, Jess!" hollered Raul, and there was more laughter. Another printer said he'd like a pound, too. Perry pulled the truck forward and jockeyed back into position again. As Jess climbed down from the cab, Harvey looked up from the press where he was working and asked Jess if he'd been driving long, and Jess half smiled at him—but there was anger in his eyes—and told him to tend to the press and he'd take care of the driving.

I grinned, enjoying the exchange, but something about it bothered me, and gnawed at the back of my mind. I couldn't put my finger on it, though.

"Got to get that baby up to Tucson and have 'em look at that low gear," Jess said to Raul. "Long as I had her she's been doing that. Still under warranty—all's I need is the time to get up there."

"Maybe they can put in rubber gears for you," suggested Harvey, and Jess shook his fist at him.

"Either that," Raul teased, "or you'd better take yourself some driving lessons."

Jess drew back his arm, as if to punch Raul, but instead swore at him in Spanish, then turned and walked to his truck.

Just then I realized what it was that bothered me—what it was about the snipe hunt that I had forgotten. Maybe it was hearing those Spanish words that put the sound into focus for me—but it was that exact same grinding-of-gears sound I had heard coming from beyond the hill the night of the snipe hunt. My knees went weak.

If it *had* been Jess's truck that night so many weeks ago, then why hadn't I heard it since? I asked myself. And then I answered myself, too. I hadn't heard it because usually when Jess shifted into low gear to pull away with the bundles of papers for Corinth and other points north, the old flatbed press was running, and it was such a noisy old clunker that it could drown out the sound of a Concorde jet flying low through the newsroom.

Harvey had the page one form in place and he signaled Raul, who punched the button that started the press running. I couldn't move. I stood there. So Jess had been transporting a human cargo of illegal aliens in that fancy truck of his, along with the bundles of the *Chronicle!* It was hard to believe.

Of course I had no proof, no way of knowing for sure. All I had to go on was the sound of the grinding gears and that sure wasn't much in the way of evidence. The press was running smoothly and there seemed to be no mechanical problems, so Harvey gave Raul the signal to speed up. The sound increased and the papers, all folded and neat, came off the press at the far end, near the door where Jess's truck was parked. The shop men would gather them in bundles of one hundred, then fasten them with baling wire and carry the bundles over to where Jess waited to load them into the truck.

I tried to think of every possibility. The number of papers he carried north Jess could load in a pickup, or even in the trunk of a car. Why the big truck? Because it was loaded with illegals? He had a perfect excuse to drive around the county without people ever becoming suspicious. Who could imagine that Jesus Perez, alias Jess Perry, ever hauled anything other than newspapers or an occasional load of furniture or freight of some sort? He had a perfect cover.

Casually as I could, I wandered over toward the truck. I'd never had much to say to Jess before because our paths really never seemed to cross. He was always parked at the rear of the *Chronicle* shop for a half hour or at most an hour every midday, but usually at that time I was up in the newsroom working on a story or listening for the telephone, or else I was over at the police station or someplace else looking for news, or maybe eating an early lunch. If I did happen to be down in the shop I was busy with Harvey or Raul or one of the other printers, and didn't have time for chitchat with Jess. Anyway, he was sort of grouchy, and not the kind of man you'd normally make small talk with. But just then I *had* to make small talk with him, and try to get a look into his truck.

Forcing a smile onto my face I told Jess that I hoped he was taking plenty of papers up to Corinth that day. "We've got a good feature story on an old, retired prospector from around there," I said to him. "Should sell plenty of papers." I pointed to the story, which ran the full eight columns across the bottom of page one, complete with a photo of the bearded miner with his arm around his faithful burro.

"Yeah," said Jess. He didn't seem too enthusiastic. One side of the rear door of the truck was open partway, and I sidled over to catch it at the right angle. Jess picked up a bundle and carried it toward the truck. I hurried ahead of him and pulled the door open, as if I was doing him a favor. I grabbed a quick look inside. There was nothing in there except the few bundles of *Chronicles* he had already loaded. No passengers. I didn't know whether to be disappointed or relieved. Maybe he wasn't hauling any human cargo this trip. Maybe he didn't carry them every time he headed north. Or maybe he picked them up somewhere after he left the *Chronicle* office. There were a lot of maybes, but that had to be it. Jess wouldn't dare stop at the newspaper to pick up his load of bundles if he had a bunch of illegal aliens in the rear of the truck. But where did he load them in the truck? That was the big question, and I had to find out the answer.

I had to follow him; there was no other way I could find out. I laughed to myself. I could just imagine my pedaling away, tailing him on the old green monster. Well, that was out. I thought about borrowing Mitch's wagon, but he had driven it to the chamber luncheon. The only other car I could think of was Bran's.

A wild thought. What if Bran actually *was* involved in the smuggling ring. Would he be willing to let me use his car to chase one of his coyote partners? I chuckled again. It *was* wild, but I had to get a car.

Upstairs, Bran was off the phone. I couldn't tell him why I needed the wheels, just in case, but I did have to tell him something.

"Bran," I said, "I need to borrow your Maverick. It's real important, but I can't tell you why."

"Have to do with *Chronicle* business?" he asked, looking at me over his glasses. I nodded. He thought for a minute, chomping on his cigar, then stood up and fished in his pocket for the car keys. Handing them to me he said, "Be careful—treat 'er nicely. She might just be a Maverick, but—"

"Yeah," I said, "I know, she has the soul of a Mercedes."

He waved his hand at me in a "get lost" motion, and I took off down the stairs. As I reached the bottom step the door opened and Mrs. Fitzhugh walked inside.

"Young man," she said, putting out her umbrella to stop me. "Trevor—is he upstairs?"

That's all I needed just then—a hassle with her. Jess must be about to pull out, if he hadn't left already. If I wanted to follow him, I had to be on my way or I'd miss him.

There was no other way to get her off my back. "Yeah," I said, "he's upstairs. I think maybe he's expecting you."

Her face brightened and she thanked me, then mounted the steps. I hurried outside and ran around the building. Poor Bran.

If he was part of the smuggling ring, he deserved Mrs. Fitzhugh. If he wasn't—well, he was a newspaperman, and he'd understand about how important it was for me to get the story.

At least I hoped he'd understand.

21

A COUPLE OF miles northwest of town on the Tucson Highway, I caught sight of Jess's truck. It was some distance ahead of me and I laid back because I didn't want to get too close for fear he'd spot me in the rearview mirror. That wouldn't do at all. How to follow a truck wasn't something I had learned in my beginning journalism class in high school. For some reason we never got into that sort of thing. Anything beyond who, what, when, where, why, and how and we were strictly on our own.

For protection I let a pickup truck with a camper mounted on it pass me, so it would be a screen between Jess's truck and the Maverick. As I had expected, when we reached the Corinth Road junction, Jess turned right. The pickup continued straight, on toward Tucson, so I eased up a little, then made the turn north toward Corinth. I missed having the pickup running interference for me, but there wasn't anything I could do about it. I slowed down to let Jess put a little more distance between us, and then I felt a bit safer.

Now that I was on the way, I wondered what I was going to do. Just stay back, of course, and keep hidden, yet try somehow to find out what Jess was up to. For all I knew, maybe he'd just deliver his papers to Corinth and return to Crandall. If that happened, well, it was a nice afternoon for a drive, even though I wasn't much in the mood for sightseeing. I had a feeling, though, that it would turn out to be more than just a sightseeing trip.

I wondered what Mitch would think when he discovered that one of the *Chronicle* people was involved in smuggling illegal aliens. He'd be furious, I knew. Then I got to wondering about Mitch. I hoped Bran wouldn't tell him I had borrowed the car, because then he'd ask me why I had borrowed it, and I still didn't want him to know I was chasing down the smuggling story. I didn't want him to worry about me and maybe make me drop the story or send me home. As it was, I was going to be leaving Crandall soon enough. Too soon, as far as I was concerned. My mind eased though, because Bran wasn't the kind of guy to blab something like that. He'd keep it to himself. Newspapermen are that way. I almost felt sorry I sicced Mrs. Fitzhugh on him—especially if he wasn't a coyote.

But then, what if Bran *was* part of the smuggling ring, along with Jess? I hoped he wasn't, and the more I thought about it, the more I realized he couldn't be. Or maybe it was that I just hoped he couldn't be.

Traffic on the Corinth Road was light and I let Jess keep well ahead of me. I didn't want him getting suspicious. His truck wasn't more than a speck far in the distance when a big white Cadillac passed me. I stepped it up a bit then, taking advantage of the Caddy, because I didn't want to lose Jess.

It didn't take the Cadillac long to lose me in its dust, and just a couple of minutes later he pulled out and passed the truck, and I eased up on the gas again. Just as we were nearing the side road that leads to the Garrity ranch, Jess dropped behind a hill and went out of sight. I reached the top of the hill and the road was a straight asphalt ribbon for as far as you could see in the distance, and there was no sign of Jess's truck. I looked over to the right then, and saw a cloud of dust on the Garrity road. Jess must have pulled off there. I couldn't figure out why.

A side road angled off the Garrity road into a heavy stand of mesquite trees beside an arroyo, I remembered. I pulled off the highway onto Mitch's road and drove slowly, so as not to raise any more dust than I had to, and pulled into that narrow side road, drew up behind a hill, and parked. The Maverick was tucked away, I was sure, and couldn't be seen from any direction. For a minute I sat trying to figure out what to do next. It wasn't many yards from the gate to the ranch buildings. I decided to avoid the road and sneak through the underbrush and climb between the strands of barbed-wire fencing, rather than open the gate. I'd have a view of all the ranch buildings from the low hill just this side of the big clearing.

Inching through the underbrush I tried to figure out why Jess stopped at the ranch. Maybe he had something to drop off there. Or, I thought—pick up. I snagged my shirt getting through the fence, but there wasn't much I could do about it. Sooner snag the shirt than my hide, I thought. Once inside the fence I dropped down on all fours and crawled through the tall grass, hoping I wouldn't come eyeball to eyeball with a rattlesnake. When I got to the top of that low hill, about twenty yards off the road, I had a full view of the ranch buildings. The truck was pulled up beside the large main door of the barn.

Larry, the hired hand, came out of the bunkhouse and walked across the open space to the barn. Jess stood at the rear of his truck. The two talked for a minute—I could hear their voices, but not what they were saying—and then Larry took a ring of keys from a clip on the side of his belt, and unlocked the big padlock on the barn door, opened it and went inside.

Jess looked around and I lowered my head, even though I was certain I was well hidden. When he was satisfied it was all clear, Jess unlocked the rear doors of the truck and swung them wide open. In a minute some men started popping out of the barn and climbing up into the truck. So Mitch's barn was where the smugglers— Larry and Jess—hid the aliens before taking them up north. The men just kept coming through the door. Their clothes were simple, the kind you'd wear to work on a farm or in a factory, and most of them carried little zipper bags or bundles or backpacks, and a few had brown grocery sacks—their belongings, packed for the journey to the promised land.

After everything I had heard and read about illegal aliens that summer, it seemed strange to be seeing some of them in real life. Really though, they didn't look any different from any other men you might happen to see on the streets of any town in the country.

Larry and Jess stood by, hurrying them along, almost as if they were herding cattle. I had just counted twenty-five men and all at once I almost yelled out, I was so surprised, because the twenty-sixth was my tire-changing friend, Vicente! At least it *looked* like Vicente. I really couldn't be positive just then. He moved fast and my view wasn't all that great because of my angle and the distance. My *amigo* Vicente an illegal alien? I didn't know what to think. After the guy who looked like Vicente there were three or four more men. I'm not positive how many, because after seeing Vicente I wasn't sure of anything.

When the last of the illegals had climbed into the truck, Jess swung the big doors shut and put the lock in place. Larry walked with him to the front of the truck and the two talked for another minute. Then Jess looked at his wristwatch and climbed up into the cab. He started the engine, shifted into low—getting that same awful grinding sound again—waved to Larry, and drove off.

So they were the smugglers—Jesus Perez and Larry Rylow. I wondered how poor Mitch would take the news when he heard that his barn was being used to hide the aliens. I hated to be the one to tell him about it, yet I supposed I'd have to do it. It was a neat operation. Jess must pick up the aliens in his truck at the border at night and drive them to the ranch and unload them in the barn. They'd wait there, I supposed, with Larry playing nursemaid, until Jess came by the next day and hauled them somewhere up north. But where? That was the big question. My job wasn't done yet. I really wanted to see the inside of that barn, but that could wait. The important thing right then was to find out how and where Jess unloaded his human freight.

When Larry had closed the barn door and was walking back toward the bunkhouse, I left my hiding place and crawled back to the car. I didn't even slam the door shut, for fear Larry would hear it, and again I drove slowly along the dirt road to keep the dust down. In a minute I was on the highway heading for Corinth. I slammed the door tight and was on my way.

I knew it wouldn't take long to catch sight of Jess, because he wouldn't be traveling very fast with all those men in the rear of his truck. I spotted him in about ten minutes and then just kept my distance, like before, and soon we arrived in Corinth. I'd never been in the town before, but it wasn't much to see. It was smaller than Crandall, and a lot older. The town was built on a bunch of hills, and some of the houses were perched on hillsides and looked as though they might start sliding down into the canyons at any moment. Corinth was a real mining town and it had sort of a rough appearance, and its streets were narrow and winding. There weren't many people around, and then I remembered that the mine there had been closed. Just then wasn't the time for me to take a rubberneck tour though, so I didn't try to take in all the sights. I was busy enough keeping an eye on Jess's truck and at the same time, not getting too close to it.

Jess drove right through the center of town and about

a block beyond what seemed to be Corinth's busiest intersection he stopped, right in the traffic lane, set the blinkers going and got out of the truck. I pulled to the curb at a yellow-painted loading zone in front of a dry-goods store and hoped that he hadn't spotted me in Bran's yellow Maverick.

From where I was parked my view wasn't all that great, but I did manage to see him open the rear of the truck just a little bit, then reach inside for one bundle of *Chronicle*s. He slammed the door again and locked it, then carried the bundle of newspapers into a store.

The sign sticking out over the sidewalk said that it was a news depot. That made sense. While he was still inside, a delivery truck pulled up behind me in the loading zone and the driver gave a couple of honks on the horn. For a few seconds I just sat there, not knowing what to do. I didn't want to pull out into the lane of traffic, because then I'd have to drive right up behind or past Jess's truck. Impatiently the driver behind me tooted again and he stuck his head out the window and hollered something at me. Quickly I flipped off the ignition and climbed out of the car and walked to the truck behind me.

"I'll be out of your way in a second," I told the driver. "Having some trouble—maybe it's vapor lock or something."

"Want me to have a look at it?" he offered.

"No thanks," I told him. "It should've cleared by now. Let me try it again."

He waved to me that he understood. I'm glad he did, because I sure didn't. I'd heard of vapor lock, but had no idea what it was, except that sometimes cars have that problem in warm weather. Just as I got back into the car, Jess came out of the news depot and drove off. I turned the key and started the Maverick, then waved to the driver behind me that all was well. He waved back. Friendly people, those Corinthians.

Pulling away from the curb and into the traffic lane, I kept at least a block behind Jess. Up ahead he turned right, and when I reached that corner, I did the same. There was no sign of him though, when I turned. I could have kicked myself for losing him after all those miles. For a few blocks I drove straight ahead, slowing down at each intersection to see if he might have turned one direction or the other. The third street up, I hit it lucky.

Jess's truck was parked about midway up the block in a residential area. I drove on past the side street, not wanting to risk being seen. I noticed that there was a pickup truck in the driveway next to his truck. I drove one more block, made a U-turn and passed the side street again, as slowly as I safely could. It looked as though Jess was handing the bundles to a man in the pickup. He must be the guy who makes home deliveries in Corinth, I guessed.

On the corner was a drive-in restaurant, and I pulled into the parking lot and slipped the Maverick between two other cars, then went inside and got a cold drink to go. From inside the restaurant I had a view up the side street where Jess was parked. When they had finished transferring the bundles into the pickup, he and the other man talked for a few minutes, then Jess got into his truck and drove on up the street. He turned right at the corner and I guessed that he would be back on that main street before too long. I was right. At the next corner he made a left onto the street and drove right past the restaurant. I stayed inside until he had passed, then hurried out to Bran's car. I was back on Jess's tail in a couple of minutes.

He drove fast through the town, but I held back, not knowing whether he had another stop to make before he unloaded his Mexican passengers. He drove straight out of town though, and headed north. I remembered from having studied the Arizona road map that the highway he was on went directly up to the Interstate, which was about twelve miles north of Corinth.

At the Interstate he got onto the eastbound access road, but instead of taking the entry ramp onto the highway itself, he stayed on the access road. After a few miles the road passed through a large stand of tall trees—cottonwoods, I think—and as he entered the grove, Jess slowed his speed. A short distance later he pulled off the road onto an unpaved one. I slowed too, but kept driving. As I passed I looked up the road and caught a glimpse of what looked like a rail fence. Not many yards beyond I found a place where I could pull off the road and hide the car. Then I started doubling back on foot through the grove of trees, toward where he had turned off. An underground river must have run right through that area, because the underbrush was thick and lush. It was probably crawling with snakes, but I didn't have any choice, so I just tromped on ahead. I'll bet Woodward and Bernstein hadn't had to worry about rattlesnakes in Washington, except for the two-legged kind. Up ahead was a clearing, where there were cattle pens, a large corral, and a couple of chutes for loading cattle into cattle trucks, only there wasn't a cow in sight.

Jess had pulled up his truck beside a rail fence, and directly behind it were parked two late-model automobiles, each with a large travel trailer hitched behind it. There were two men there, too, both wearing sport shirts and caps, looking just like any tourists you'd be likely to see on the highways. The spot was perfect for what they were up to. It was completely surrounded by trees, and probably couldn't be seen by cars passing on the Interstate or any of the nearby side roads. Jess didn't waste any time.

Quickly he unlocked the rear doors of his truck and swung them wide open. He called out something in Spanish to the men inside, and they started dropping off the back of the truck.

I held my breath and watched. Sure enough, the sixth guy out of the truck was Vicente. He still had that grease spot on his pants. I wanted to call out to him, to tell him hello, to ask how he'd been, to wish him luck. But of course I couldn't. I wished he'd taken that five dollar bill that night because it might've helped him a little bit if he had to pay hundreds of dollars to get smuggled up north someplace. But Vicente was proud, I knew. He couldn't take money for helping a friend. Good luck, *amigo mio*, I thought. Practice that English. I wished I could have told Vicente that, instead of just thinking it.

The first dozen men went to the far trailer, and climbed into it through a side door, and the rest of the Mexican men got into the second trailer. Before the drivers shut the doors, I could see that the insides of the trailers had been pretty well stripped, so that the passengers would have plenty of room to stretch out on the floor inside. I crept closer for a better look, wishing I had thought to bring a camera with me.

Then I happened to think of license numbers. I took my small notebook from a hip pocket and with a ballpoint pen wrote a description of both cars and trailers. From where I was hiding I could make out the license plates only on the trailers—both had Illinois plates—but couldn't see those on the autos at all. Carefully I crawled through the high grass, past the auto-trailer rigs, until I was in front of the autos. From there I could make out the auto tags, too. I tucked away the notebook and pen and began backing up slowly when my left foot snapped a dry, dead mesquite branch. It sounded like a cannon being shot off. Jess and the other two men quickly turned my way.

I sucked in my breath and held it.

The three of them started moving toward me and I knew then that I had had it. The grasses and underbrush made good cover for me from a distance, but up close was a different matter. My heart was beating faster than it ever had in my whole life and I felt weak all over. I tried to think of what to do, and running was the best idea I could come up with. But suppose they were faster than I was, and of course, if I got up and ran, Jess would see me. The way my body felt, all weak and limp, I wondered if it would run if my head told it to.

Well, I hoped it would, because it was now or never.

Jess and the two drivers kept coming and they couldn't have been more than thirty feet from me by that time. I needed at least that much of a head start if I was going to outrace them.

I had to run. There was nothing else I could do but stay put, and I wasn't about to do that. I tried to dig my toes into the ground for a good, fast start, and drew up my knees and tensed myself. I was as set as I'd ever be.

22

THE UNITED STATES Cavalry came to my rescue.

Well, not really the cavalry—just a couple of ranch kids on horseback. They couldn't have been more than ten or eleven years old, and they appeared suddenly at the edge of the clearing, driving a fat steer ahead of them. Now I know how the settlers felt when the Indians were closing in on the wagon train and all of a sudden the cavalry came riding over the hill with flags flying and bugles blaring.

Jess laughed out loud, shook his head and turned away from me, heading toward the vehicles. The other two men followed him. "There's your noise," he said. "Kids on horses."

"Had me worried for a minute," said one of the drivers.

They all exchanged howdys as the boys rode through. Then Jess looked at his watch and told the men they'd better be on their way. He waited until the two auto-trailer rigs had gone out of sight, then he got into the truck and drove off, too.

For about ten minutes I stayed in my hiding place, and

when I figured it was all clear, I got up and walked back to the car. I didn't want to drive all the way back to Crandall worrying about overtaking Jess, so in Corinth I stopped and bought a hamburger for late lunch, then headed for home. It was almost four o'clock when I got back to the *Chronicle* newsroom, and I was relieved to see that Mitch wasn't around. Bran was there though, and I was afraid he'd ask me where I had been with his Maverick all afternoon, because I sure didn't want to tell him, in case he did happen to be part of the smuggling ring. I needn't have worried.

"That woman," he said, shaking his head. "That woman."

"What woman?"

"Fitzhugh—who else? She came up those stairs just after you left. Had a story about some Ladies Aid benefit she's in charge of, and would you believe it, she dictated the story to me, word for word, just the way she wants it to appear in the *Chronicle*." Bran stood, walked around his desk, picked up his ruler and flung it at the U.S. map on the far wall. It hit North Dakota.

"Mark, I couldn't get away. She had me cornered and she held me there. I kept hoping I'd hear a siren that I could chase, or that I'd get an important telephone call or that the president of the United States would walk into the newsroom and ask me to interview him." He dropped into his chair and propped his heels on the space bar of his typewriter.

"No such luck. The president didn't show up—damned if I'll ever vote for *him* again. Not even a Crandall city councilman stepped into the newsroom. There's never a councilman around when you really need one. Why, nobody came in to save me, there weren't any sirens and the blasted telephone didn't ring once. I didn't have even the slightest excuse to get away from her."

"Gee, Bran," I said, "I'm sorry. I really am."

"Believe me, Mark—you're not half as sorry as I am. It was awful. I just sat there taking notes and smiling and nodding and she asked me to come to dinner at her place tonight and I went on smiling and nodding and—six o'clock."

"Six o'clock, what?" I asked.

"Six o'clock dinner. I accepted her invitation without even realizing what I was doing."

Bran ignored my laugh.

"I nodded and smiled my way right into it and there was no way I could back out. I was trapped. You won't catch *me* nodding and smiling again."

"I'll bet she's a great cook though," I said. "She seems the type."

"She is—that's the problem. Sets a fine table and that's her trap."

"Well, you'd better get home and shower. You don't want to be late, Bran. By the way, thanks for the use of the car. I put a couple of dollars' worth of gas in it before I parked it in the lot." I handed him the keys.

"Get what you were after?" he asked.

I told him I did and he didn't press for more information. Then I asked if Mitch had wondered where I was that afternoon.

"Mitch didn't show up this afternoon," said Bran. "It was just me here. And *her!*"

Bran left and I wished him luck with Mrs. Fitzhugh and told him to have a good time. He turned his head my way and gave me a dirty look, then went down the stairs, grumbling to himself.

For a long time I sat at my desk, trying to sort things out in my mind. At that point I didn't know what to do next, who to turn to, how to handle the information I had dug up. Everything had happened so quickly that afternoon, from the second I heard the grinding gears of Jess's truck. It was so long ago, that night of the snipe hunt, that I was surprised I'd remember something small like that, like the weird sound of grinding gears.

As far as clues go, that one was pretty stupid, yet it had led me on the right track. If I hadn't been down there in the shop and if Jess hadn't backed his truck in crooked and if the guys hadn't teased him about his driving and if the press had already started and if I hadn't gone snipe hunting that first night in Crandall and if—*if*. Everything was "if" just then. It was the big word. But what should I do next? That's what I kept asking myself. About all I knew for sure was that Vicente had gotten away. My friend was safe. At least I hoped he was safe.

I thought about going to Mitch right away and telling him how Jess and Larry were smuggling aliens into this country and were using his barn to hide them in. It would be an awful shock for Mitch, I realized, but he had to know about it right away. But then I got to thinking that before I told him, I'd like to know more of the details and have the whole thing wrapped up and tied in a nice package, all ready to print on the front page of the

Chronicle. That would mean more digging though, and time was running out for me.

What I really needed was more luck, like I had had that afternoon, but you can't make luck happen just because you'd like it to. Maybe I should talk it over with someone. Tomas—he'd be the perfect one, of course. He'd be able to give me advice. Or maybe even Wally Sternaman would, for that matter. I was still ticked off at Wally and I'm sure he felt the same way toward me, but after all, I had some information—some solid information—that would help him wind up his case. Maybe Wally *was* the one to go to. While I was considering that, the phone rang. It was Shannon.

"Where are you?" I asked.

"Downstairs," she said. "I've been up there so many times this afternoon looking for you that I didn't want to waste any more energy on those stairs if you weren't there. Don't go away."

She had no more than hung up the phone when I heard her footsteps on the stairs. Shan popped into the newsroom, a silly grin on her face, and looked around.

"Everybody's gone," I told her.

"But I didn't come up to see *everybody*—I came up to see *you!*" She ran across the newsroom, skirted around my desk, jumped up and landed on my lap. My swivel chair rolled half a foot, then one of the wheels broke and the chair tossed us like a dump truck. We landed in the pile of out-of-town newspapers stacked behind my desk.

"You're mad!" I said. "A wild woman!" We were sprawled on the floor and I was choking and laughing and gasping for air, all at once, and Shannon raised her head and kissed me.

"Where *have* you been all afternoon, Matthew?" she asked, looking down at me, her elbows planted on my chest.

"Just out driving, mostly," I told her, feeling as foolish as I'd ever felt in my life. "What if somebody comes up those stairs?" I asked.

"You'll just have to tell them the office is closed—it's after five—and to come back tomorrow."

"That's not what I mean," I said. "What if your dad comes in and sees us?"

"He won't," she said, tickling the tip of my nose with a long fingernail. "He and Mom are having dinner guests tonight and I don't want to eat with them. Why don't we go out for Mexican food? I'll treat!"

"How can I go anywhere with you sitting on top of me?"

"Well, if you'll promise to go to dinner I'll let you get up. Promise?"

There were a lot of things I wanted to do that night, like talking with Tomas or Wally, going over my notes, getting everything that had happened that day down on paper, but all of a sudden everything else seemed unimportant. Besides, I'd accomplished enough for one day.

"Okay—I promise."

Shan leaned over, gave me a quick peck on the cheek, jumped up and offered me a hand. I got slowly to my feet. How neither one of us had been hurt when the chair broke, I'll never know. Lucky, I guess. The rest of the building was locked, so I turned out all the newsroom lights except for the one in the hallway that we left burning at night, and we went downstairs and I let us out the front door and locked it after us.

I pedaled the bike back to my hotel so I'd have it next morning, and Shan went home in the wagon to get ready; then she picked me up an hour later. I was glad we were going to eat early. That would give me time, after Shannon went home, to go to the police station and have Tomas meet me. I had decided I owed it to Tomas to tell him what I had found out and ask him what I should do next. I trusted Tomas and knew that with his police background, he'd be able to give me some good advice.

We went to a restaurant that Shan said 'most everybody thought had the best Mexican food in southern Arizona. "Even people from La Pizca go there to eat," she said. It was a little bit hokey, but a pleasant place with Mexican music playing in the background. The restaurant was decorated with piñatas and draped serapes and some sombreros, along with blowups of old pictures of Mexican revolutionary heroes and old bull-fight posters.

It was early and we almost had the place to ourselves. We had been laughing and silly when the chair broke in the office, but now it was all changed. Both of us tried to be cheerful over dinner, but it didn't work out very well. I kept thinking, and I guess Shan did, too, that in less than a week I'd be leaving Crandall. We tried to make jokes and say silly things, but it all fell flat. Nothing seemed very funny. About the only real laugh we had was when I told Shan about how Mrs. Fitzhugh had cornered Bran and invited him to dinner and he had accepted before he realized what was happening.

I kept thinking, too, about what had happened that afternoon—how suddenly my investigation of the smuggling ring had come alive again, had blossomed out, really—and I wanted to tell Shan all about it and share it with her, but I knew I couldn't talk to even her about it until after I told Tomas.

The most exciting thing that happened at dinner was when I tangled with some *salsa*—Mexican hot sauce—that just about burned my tongue off. I had spooned some of the *salsa* onto my taco and Shan made a worried face and said I should go easy because it was really highly seasoned, but I pooh-poohed her and said that was okay, because I liked my Mexican food hot. Ha!

I should have listened to her. It was the hottest thing I'd had in my mouth all my life. My tongue burned and I guess my face went red and I started crying. Not really crying, but the tears streamed down my face. I reached for my water glass and emptied it and then I drained my iced-tea glass and shook the ice into my mouth and sucked on it, but nothing helped. It still burned. I grabbed Shan's glass of water and drank it, too.

"You've got it bad, guy," she said. At least she didn't say she had told me so. Shan wasn't that kind. She ripped open an envelope of sugar from the sugar bowl in the middle of the table and poured all of it into a spoon and handed it to me.

"Too much sugar isn't good for you," she said,

sounding like somebody's mother, "but put all of this in your mouth at once and hold it in there and roll your tongue around in it."

Almost at once the burning began to taper off, and before long my mouth was almost back to normal. "Where did you learn that?" I asked. She shrugged and shook her head.

"Gosh, I don't know. I guess I've always known it—it's one of those things you just grow up knowing."

"But I didn't grow up knowing it."

"Of course not, you haven't been eating Mexican food all your life, either," she said. "I guess that's the difference. Anything sweet—sugar, a piece of candy—will cool your tongue when the Mexican food gets too spicy."

I looked at her across the table and realized that I had to be the luckiest guy in all Arizona. Shannon Garrity was beautiful, probably the most beautiful girl I had ever known. Her long, blonde hair was like a waterfall of honey in that dim light of the restaurant, and it was golden against her suntanned face. I noticed, though, that the gray of her eyes was deeper that night than usual. It was almost as if they were troubled, or sad.

Through the rest of the meal we talked, but we didn't really say anything. Just small talk, just words to keep the silence from growing up between us. Both of us avoided mentioning the one thing that was most on our minds. Neither of us wanted to talk about that, so we talked about everything but.

The tables around us began filling up and soon after we

finished eating we decided to leave. I asked Shan if she wanted to go to the movies and she said she didn't. She'd rather just talk.

"We don't have many evenings left to be together," she said. "I'd rather just be with you—no movies or anything. Just us." That was exactly the way I felt, too.

"There are some clouds—that means it's going to be a nice sunset," I said. "Why don't we go out to where we watched that sunset?" She liked the idea and I was glad, because if there was any one place in Crandall that meant something special to me, that was it. The Hill, where we had parked after the dance and looked at the lights of the twin cities was a good place, too, but our own sunset spot was better.

We parked and found the same outcropping of rock, and sat with our backs against the same boulder, and we watched the same show of oranges and pinks we had watched that other evening, but somehow it wasn't quite the same. The sunset colors seemed paler than they had been that other evening, or maybe it was just my imagination playing tricks on me. Maybe they just seemed less vivid, less brilliant, than the colors in the sunset I remembered, because now I was feeling sad about leaving, and I knew there wouldn't be many more sunsets for us to share.

"What day is this?" Shan asked, leaning her head back on my shoulder.

"Monday."

"And you leave. . . ."

"Saturday. As soon as the Saturday edition goes to

press your Dad's going to drive me to Tucson. I'll catch a late afternoon flight."

"Stay over a day, Winky. Just till Sunday. That would give us one more evening together."

"I have my reservation—"

"You can change it. Change it for me?"

"I'll see," I said. "I'll call the airline tomorrow. We'll have to see if your father can drive me up on Sunday. I know he was figuring on Saturday."

"Daddy's real flexible and I know he and Mom would like to have you around for another day."

"We'll see how it works out," I said.

We sat quietly for a while and then Shannon tried to talk me into going to the University of Arizona instead of Northwestern. She said the U of A had a good journ department, too. "And," said Shan, "we'd be together."

"I'd like that," I said, "you know I would. But for years I've had my heart set on Northwestern. Medill School of Journalism is one of the best."

"Then maybe *I* could go *there*," she said brightly. "I suppose I'll just have to work on Mom and Dad. I'll try to wear 'em down and they'll be so happy to get rid of me that they'll send me anywhere."

Both of us laughed, but the laughter was phony because we both knew that it probably wouldn't ever happen.

I had dated a lot of girls back home and some of them I liked a lot, but no girl I had ever known was like Shan. Shan, I loved, and I had never loved any girl before. I told her so, and she raised her mouth to be kissed.

"This summer—" she said softly, "it's gone by so

quickly. I don't want it to end, Winky. I don't want you to get on that plane and go home and leave me."

"We'll be together again soon, Shannie," I said. "Who knows? Maybe your family can come to our place at Christmastime for a visit. I know my folks would love to have you all, and I could show you everything back there. . . ."

"I'd like that," she said. "I really would."

There was no more color left in the sky and it was quickly going black. We didn't have a flashlight with us and soon we'd have to head for the car.

"I'll always remember this place," I told her, and she said she would, too.

"When I get lonely for you, Winky, I'm going to come here just to think about you, and when I get your letters I'll bring them here to read. It'll be almost as though we're together," she said. "Almost. . . ." She let the word drift into the night, and she sobbed then and I wiped at her tears with my thumb.

For a minute I didn't say anything because I was afraid that if I did, I would crack, too.

"It's not fair, Matt, for you to go home, for you to leave. The summer's been too good to end and it shouldn't have to."

"You're right," I said. "It's not fair." And then I asked her if she had a picture she could give me, and she said she didn't have a good one, but that she'd have Charlie Prentiss take one. "I'll send it up to you," she promised, "if you'll give me one."

"I have a school yearbook picture that's not all that great, but it's at home. I'll send it in my first letter." We kissed again, and then again, and then we sat holding each other as the night sky deepened. I lost track of time.

"We'd better try to find the car," I said finally, and Shannon nodded. I stood up and helped her to her feet and we took a few steps and she stopped and raised her arms and laced her fingers behind my neck.

"Maybe," she said brightly, "maybe next summer you could come out here and work on the *Chronicle* again, Winky. I'll talk to Daddy and see what he says." She drew my face down to hers.

The idea of another summer with Shannon sounded wonderful, I thought as we kissed, except that next summer was such a long time off. A lot of things could happen before then, but I didn't want to say that.

"Yeah," I answered between kisses, "maybe next summer."

23

SHANNON DROPPED ME at the Railroad Hotel. I was tired and toyed with the idea of going to bed and talking with Tomas the next day. I wish I had.

I would have enjoyed the sleep a lot more than I enjoyed getting beat up.

It's just a couple of blocks' walk from the Railroad Hotel to the police station and part of it follows a side business street that isn't lighted at all after dark, except for a few small night-lights in some of the shops. I'd walked that stretch dozens of times during the summer and never thought anything about it. In Crandall people didn't worry about things like dark streets. I should have been worrying, though.

Just after I passed the old two-story red brick building that used to be the feed-and-grain store, but that had been standing empty for years, they jumped me. I had been thinking and my mind was miles away, so they took me completely by surprise. Beside the red brick building there was an empty lot and as I walked past it somebody jumped me from behind and threw a strong arm around my chest, pinning my arms to my side, and clamped his other hand over my mouth. It happened so quickly that he had me halfway into the empty lot before I could fight back. I dragged my feet and then kicked backward at him, but it did no good.

I wanted to cry out, but with his hand over my mouth, yelling was out of the question. I struggled and tried to shake myself free, but whoever was holding me was about ten times stronger than I am. The more I struggled, the tighter he held. I kicked backward some more, but I was wearing sneakers and sneakers are not what you would call deadly weapons. I don't think I even connected once with his shins.

Dragging me back further from the sidewalk, he finally released the hand over my mouth and I started to yell. Quickly the hand slapped back in place and when it did it felt as though I lost a handful of teeth. The fingers and the thumb dug deep into my cheeks and I could taste the salt of blood in my mouth. My blood!

Suddenly there was a shadowy figure in front of me—that made two of them—darker than the darkness of the Arizona night. A hand came out and grabbed my shirt and twisted. Then a fist shot out of the darkness and caught me right where my enchiladas and tacos were. Again I tried to yell out, but the hand over my mouth muffled any sound I might've made. My nose was clogged and I gasped for breath. I jerked my head to one side and for a second was free of the hand and I sucked in sharp breaths, trying to fill my lungs.

The hand was over my mouth again, and a knee was in my back. My stomach felt as though I had a lead ball in it and for a minute I thought I was going to throw up. My knees were weak and my heart was thunking like a car rolling downhill on four flat tires and my temples were throbbing. I had never been more afraid in my life. I jerked my head free again and blurted out, "My wallet's in my back pocket!" There wasn't much money in it, but what was there, they were welcome to. The figure in front of me reached out and slapped me across the face and told me to keep my money.

Back snapped my head, and my face stung from the slap. The more I tried to wriggle loose, the tighter the arm became around my middle. Someone had hold of my hair then, and was pulling my head backward. I wanted to cry out but knew that would only bring the hand back over my mouth and that I could do without.

"Then what *do* you want?" I gasped between breaths and a fist caught me again in the gut and I vomited right down my shirt front. The man holding me swung me back and forth, like I was a rag doll, and then he let go of my hair and with that hand, punched me in the kidneys. I saw stars. I fought to keep from crying, but the fight was a losing one. The tears poured from my eyes and my body jerked with sobs.

"Tell me what you want!" I bawled out and the two men laughed. In the very pale light from a lamppost in the next block I caught a glimpse of the man facing me, though it didn't help. He had a woman's stocking drawn over his head, and his face was an eerie, doughy mass.

"Forget it," said the man in front of me. There was a strong Spanish accent in his voice. "Lay off this smuggling thing you're nosing into, hear?" And he hit me again in the middle. Instead of answering, I took a deep sniff and cleared my nose. He slapped me and asked again if I understood, and I nodded.

"It's something don't concern you!" I listened carefully to the voice, trying to place it. Was it Jess? No, it had a completely different tone to it from Jess's voice. I would have known Jess's voice in a second.

"Just you mind your own business!" said the man who was holding me. That was the first thing he had said, and his voice didn't sound familiar, either. It had a Spanish accent, too. So both of the men who were working me over were strangers. I had no idea who they were, but for sure they knew who *I* was!

I knew better than to argue, so I just said, "Yeah," and nodded and then sniffed again to clear my nose. At last I got some breath through it and also a noseful of something that smelled sweet. Sweet and familiar. I tried to remember where it was I had smelled that sickeningly sweet smell and I didn't have to think very hard.

It was Larry, of course. Mitch's hired hand! It wasn't Larry who was holding me, or who had been hitting me, but he was around, somewhere close by. Nobody else but Larry would wear that awful, sweet-smelling stuff on his hair. Ever since I saw him at Mitch's barn, letting the illegals out to climb into Jess's truck, I had just supposed he was a little guy, a punk in the operation, but now I realized he was a big one. Maybe *the* big one—*numero uno*, as Wally had called him. Obviously he was in charge here, even though he was keeping out of sight.

All the struggle and fight had gone out of me, and I

had decided that if I tried to shake loose or swing out at them, it would be just that much tougher on me, so I let myself go limp. The guy behind me had to hold me up.

"You got the message, kid?" the other one asked, and I half-whispered, "Yeah." He gave me a karate chop in the arm, just below the shoulder, and I thought my arm was going to fall off. Then he followed through with a knee to my stomach.

"Okay—remember!" and all at once the man behind me let loose and I sprawled to the ground. The two ran off toward the alley and I heard car doors slamming and then the sound of tires spinning on dirt. I could see a dark shadow move across the open space, and once it was behind the next building I saw the glow of head-lights suddenly come on.

For at least five minutes, I didn't even try to move. It would have done no good. I lay there, parts of my body aching, other parts throbbing. I was sore all over, and sweaty and hot. I tried to think of what to do next. I couldn't go to the police station looking as I imagined I must look. That would bring up too many questions I didn't want to answer just then. I took some deep breaths and got to my feet and aimed them in the direction of the hotel. The smell of my own vomit almost gagged me and I breathed through my mouth. At the hotel I went in the back entrance and up the back stairs, so no one would see me. I stopped in my room only long enough to empty my pockets, get some clean underwear, a shirt and Levi's, and then went down the hall to the bathroom.

I kicked off my sneakers and pulled the socks from my

feet, and then, still fully dressed, stepped into the shower and stood under the spray. When my shirt was rinsed off I unbuttoned it and threw it aside and then did the same with my pants. When I was naked I stood under the shower letting the water run all over me, and finally turned the handle slowly until the water was ice cold.

As I toweled myself I looked into the mirror and was surprised to see that I looked better than I had expected. My face was red in places, from the slaps and the hand that had been clamped over my mouth, and my upper lip was puffy, but not much. By morning I'd probably look normal. I wrung out my clothes, hurried to my room and dressed quickly. On the way to the lobby I stopped at the ice machine and grabbed a couple of cubes and held them on my swollen lip as I walked to the pay phone. The coffee shop was closed and there was no one in the lobby except for the night clerk, an old man who was dozing behind the front desk.

I dialed the police station and asked the desk sergeant to radio Tomas and ask him to pick me up at the hotel. I said it was important. I hung on for a few minutes and then the sergeant was back on the line. He said Duarte would be at the hotel in five minutes; he was there in three.

As we slowly cruised the downtown streets, I told Tomas everything. He didn't say a single word until I had finished. Then he pulled to the curb and flicked on the dome light.

"Let me have a look at you, Matt," he said. With his fingertips he gently touched my face here and there, pausing a few times to ask, "That hurt?"

I told him no, that the face took only slaps. "They saved the fists for the gut and the kidneys."

"I'm sorry, horse," he said. "Think anything's broken? Think we should drop by at the hospital and let them have a look at you in the emergency room?"

"No," I said. "I think I was scared more than I was hurt. By morning I'll be okay. I know I will."

Tomas turned off the dome light in the car and pulled away from the curb. He lifted the microphone from the clamp beneath the dash, pushed the button and called the police station.

"I'll be out of service for a while," he told the sergeant. "Official business—let one of the other units cover for me, but if you need me you can probably reach me by phone at border patrol."

In less than five minutes we were sitting in a back office of the border patrol headquarters building, which is just a few yards from the crossing into La Pizca. After the border patrolman on duty had radioed Wally in the field, he poured coffee for Tomas and me, and we drank it out of plastic cups as we waited.

It wasn't long before Wally Sternaman and his partner Fred Thede walked into the office. They didn't seem too happy to see me.

"This better be good," Wally told Tomas as he perched on the edge of a desk. Fred poured coffee from the big urn in the corner and gave Wally a cup and kept one for himself.

"It's plenty good," Tomas said. "Looks as though Matt here has broken your ring—the big one. Picked up a few lumps along the way, but nothing he won't get over."

Wally took a sip of coffee, then walked around behind the desk. "You want to tell me about it, Matt?"

"Any time," I said, "just so you make sure we get the story first for the *Chronicle*."

Fred Thede laughed. "You newspaper guys—all you ever think about is your stories."

Wally ignored him. "Mind if I tape it?" he asked, pointing to the Sony cassette recorder on his desk. I said that would be fine with me. He checked the tape in the recorder, flipped the "on" switch and, for the second time in an hour, I told my story, not leaving out a single detail. I told it almost as I planned to write it when the time came. Wally made some notes as I talked, and when I was done he didn't have a single question to ask. Raising his eyebrows, Wally looked over at Fred Thede, then at Tomas, then back at me.

"Sounds solid to me, Matt," said Wally. "I think we can move on it." Then he double-checked the license numbers and descriptions of those trailers and the cars pulling them, wrote it all on a piece of paper and handed the paper to Fred. Fred went over to a desk in a corner and used the telephone. I couldn't hear what he said, but I guessed he was putting out information to some law enforcement agency to try to find those cars and trailers. Suddenly I thought about Vicente again. I really felt awful about him. I hoped somehow he would get away. In my mind I kept trying to picture Vicente the way he had been that night over in La Pizca when the three of us did that silly skipping, but it didn't work. Instead I kept seeing him climbing out of Jess Perry's truck.

"How many people do we have on tonight?" Wally asked the communications man, who had been listening quietly through my whole story.

"Eleven in the field—I make twelve."

"Any of them working anything so hot they can't be called in?"

The radio man shook his head. "Slow night," he said.

"Well, phone Tremain first—he'll want to get down here, too—and if he gives the okay, call the men in from the field."

Then Wally came over to where I was sitting. "Matt, we thank you," he said. "Sorry I got bitchy with you the other night, but. . . ."

"I understand. You guys have your jobs, I have mine."

"Glad you feel that way," Wally said. "Tomas—you want to see to it Matt gets home safely?"

Nodding, Tomas stood and looked over at me. "You mean I can't tag along with you?" I asked.

Shaking his head, Wally said he was afraid I couldn't. "Company policy," he joked.

"Oh, come on now," I argued. "I just told you everything I learned about this thing—I've been crawling through the desert and following trucks and watching illegal aliens get loaded like cattle and I've been getting beat up and—surely I've earned the chance to be with you when you—well, when you move in for the kill."

Wally laughed, but it was a kind, understanding laugh.

"Wish we could take you, Matt. Really I do, but there's no way. The Uncle is pretty touchy about this sort of thing. Besides, we aren't even sure we'll move on it tonight."

I looked over at Tomas Duarte and he shrugged and shook his head. "Come on, Matt," he said. "I'll drive you home."

There was no arguing with Wally, I could see that. "You promise you'll give me the story first thing tomorrow?"

"First thing," Wally said. "Soon as we have it all put together—loose ends, and all—we'll stop by the *Chronicle* office and give you the story. It's yours—that's a promise."

That made me feel better. Not much, but a little bit.

"Good luck," I told Wally, and he thanked me. "I don't know who they are, but I just hope you get those guys who worked me over tonight."

Wally laughed. "We'll try," he said. "And Matt— thanks. A good job. One thing though, don't mention anything about all this to anyone until you hear from us, understand?" I told him I understood.

"Happy hunting, fella," Tomas told Wally, and I followed Tomas outside. Neither of us had much to say as we drove back to the hotel. A thousand thoughts were racing through my mind as we moved along the night-time streets of Crandall.

I thought about how I would write the lead on my story, how pleased and proud Mitch and Bran would be to break the story in the *Chronicle*. And I thought about what a fluke the whole thing had been. Me—getting my big story, just because I was a stupid city kid who had never been snipe hunting before.

And Shannon. What would she think? She'd be proud, too. That much I knew for sure. And she'd be happy it was all over, because that meant we'd be able to spend every evening together until I left. I could hardly wait to tell her.

I got to thinking then, about Vicente and the other aliens I had seen that afternoon, being loaded into the truck and then unloaded at the cattle pens, and then loaded again into the travel trailers. What about them? What would happen to them? That's what made me feel bad. It was those men, like Vicente, the poor people from down in Mexico who were trying to make better lives for themselves, who I felt sorry for. It was a tremendous problem and I hoped that someday it could be worked out. I hoped so. But those smugglers—*them* I didn't feel sorry for at all.

As Tomas pulled to the curb in front of the hotel he turned on the spotlight mounted on the police car. He played the beam around the porch of the hotel and alongside the building, then into the bushes in front of the porch. "Looks clear," he said. "Want me to walk up to your room with you?"

Just his suggestion that there might be more danger sent a chill down my back. But I told Tomas no, that I wasn't worried, and then I thanked him. He reached out his hand and clasped mine.

"Good job, horse," he told me. "Didn't think you'd do it, to be real honest, but you showed me." Smiling, he grasped my hand firmly.

It wasn't until I was in my room and had stripped down that it really hit me. I had been afraid, of course, while those two guys were roughing me up, but all at once the fear hit me again, and my whole body trembled. I made sure the door was locked and then I propped the back of the chair beneath the doorknob. I was tired. I don't think I'd ever been more tired in my life, because it had been a long and busy and exciting and frightening day. Totally washed out, I fell into bed.

But when I closed my eyes and tried to sleep, the sleep wouldn't come. My mind kept taking me back to that empty lot next to the old feed-and-grain store, and it was like a nightmare, except that I was wide awake.

24

IT WAS MIDMORNING before Wally Sternaman showed up in the *Chronicle* newsroom. I was beginning to worry that maybe he had forgotten me. I should have known better. From the minute I arrived in the office at seven o'clock, I had wanted to tell Mitch and Bran all about how I had broken the alien smuggling ring and gotten my big story. When you have good news like that you like to share it. But I had promised Wally I'd sit on it and wouldn't tell a soul, so I sat on it. It wasn't easy.

After having so little sleep the night before, I was sure I'd be punchy and walk around all day like I was in a daze, but it was just the opposite. I must have been running on excitement, because I felt bubbly and in high gear. I wasn't as sore, either, as I had expected. My lower back though, where I had been kidney-punched, was tender. Those two really must have known their job, because in the mirror that morning my face looked no worse or better than usual. It bore no marks of the beating. The redness was gone and the ice had kept down the swelling on my lip.

As always I had stopped at the police station and

checked the reports and made my notes. I was surprised to see my name on one of the case reports. It was, "Assault, aggravated," and it told how I had been attacked on the sidewalk, dragged into the empty lot and beaten by two male subjects, masked, identities unknown. It was a weird feeling, seeing my name on a police report, but I was relieved that Tomas hadn't mentioned *why* I had been assaulted. He was sitting on it, too, just as Wally had asked.

Shannon was at her desk when I entered the *Chronicle* office and walked into the first-floor lobby. She saw me and came over to the counter, her face all smiles.

"How do you feel about pork roast with oven-browned potatoes?" she asked.

"You're cuter," I told her.

"Well, I should hope so—but for second choice, pork roast? Mom took it out of the freezer this morning for dinner tonight and she told me to invite you."

"You're on," I said. "How about after dinner?"

"A walk, maybe? Or a ride? We could go up the Hill."

"Forget the pork roast. Let's just go up the Hill."

Shannon laughed. "I'll pick you up at six," she said. "Don't dress formally—the Garritys are being casual tonight."

"I wish you'd told me before—I already rented a tux for the occasion and paid cash!"

"Then wear it—I'll be in blue-jean cutoffs and one of Daddy's old shirts."

"Will an orchid clash with the color of the shirt, or would you prefer something else?"

"Oh, yellow sweetheart roses—they're my very favorite, Winky. I can't *stand* orchids. Orchids are so old ladyish. And be sure to—" Her telephone rang and she shrugged and reached for it. "Sorry," she mouthed.

"That's okay," I told her, "I've got to get upstairs, anyway." For a second though, my feet wouldn't move. I stood anchored to the spot, my eyes on Shannon, enjoying the view. She looked up as she spoke on the phone, and her eyes met mine and the warm look she tossed my way about melted me. Then I remembered the newsroom and my pocketful of notes and the alien smuggling story I hoped to be able to write that day, and I made for the stairs.

Halfway up the steps I paused and chuckled. Maybe I *should* rent a tux for dinner. Shan would just collapse and Aunt Beth and Mitch would get a kick out of it, too. A tux and my old sneakers, the dirty ones with holes in them. At lunch I'd stop by at the Master & Mister Men's Wear Shop—they rented formal wear—and find out how much it would cost to rent a tuxedo or maybe even white tie and tails. It would be a real kick.

Mitch was working desk that day and when I stepped into the newsroom Bran had the telephone propped to his ear and he was doing his rat-tat-tat machine-gun thing on the typewriter. Even after working with him all summer, his speed at three-finger typing still amazed me. He had to be the fastest typist in all Arizona. Maybe even the world. Mitch and I traded "good mornings," and Bran nodded at me without looking up and continued typing.

"Hear you tangled with some *salsa* last night," Mitch said, leaning back in his swivel chair and capping his hands on his head.

"Wow," I said, "I really did. My mouth's still a bit

sensitive. Lucky thing Shan was with me—she taught me to use sugar. Great first aid."

Mitch chuckled, then asked what I had on tap for that day's paper. I told him what stories I had picked up at the police station—nothing really big—and said I'd probably have them all written within half an hour.

He scribbled notes on a piece of copy paper so he'd remember what stories to expect from me, then he asked me to give Herb Otto a call down at his garage to see if the Pioneer Days committee was going to meet that week and if so, write a short item on it. "And then phone the funeral home and see if they have the information yet for the Newman obit. Like to get that in today," he added. Then Mitch handed me two press releases from the state agriculture department—both about cotton— and asked me to do a couple of grafs on each.

I got right at the police stories. All of them were simple, straight news, and I whipped through them in twenty minutes. They wouldn't win any prizes for me in the state press-club competition, but I was far from ashamed of them.

Herb Otto was off fishing so I wouldn't be able to get the Pioneer Days story, and I was right in the middle of dialing the funeral home when Wally Sternaman and Fred Thede came up the steps and walked into the newsroom. When I saw them my heart skipped a beat. Several beats. They hadn't forgotten me after all. I hung up the phone and told them good morning. Both looked as though they had been up half the night, too.

"How's the newspaper business?" asked Fred after they had told us all good morning.

"Not bad," Mitch answered. "Looks as though we're going to get a paper out today. How's the border-patrol business?"

Wally shrugged and sort of half-grinned. "Busy," he said. " 'Course, with us, it never slows down. It just gets busier."

"What brings you gents here?" asked Bran without taking his cigar from his mouth.

"Well, it's Matt here we've come to see," said Wally. He stumbled a couple of times saying those few words and I couldn't understand why. Probably because he's so tired, I thought.

"Can I go ahead and write the story?" I asked him.

Bran and Mitch both perked up and looked interested. It was the first either had known I was working on a border-patrol story.

"It's clear with us," Wally said.

"Did you—did you make the arrests last night?" He nodded.

"About got 'em all," Fred Thede put in.

"*About?*" I asked. "*Didn't* you get all of them?"

Wally cleared his throat. "Still a few more arrests to make—a few loose ends to tie up. Otherwise the story's all set for you to write, Matt."

The excitement grew inside me and about burst. I fought hard to keep my cool as I reached for a pencil and paper to make some notes. "You'll have to fill me in on the details," I told Wally. He sighed and sat down in the chair beside my desk. Thede sat on the table across the room and swung his feet beneath it. They exchanged odd glances. Bran stood and came around his desk and leaned back against it, his arms crossed over his chest. He and Mitch both looked strange, as if they didn't understand what was happening. They'd know soon enough.

"Well, thanks to your help, Matt, we hit it lucky—luckier then we had even hoped," Wally began.

"It's got to be one of the biggest, most sophisticated, most lucrative smuggling operations we've ever broken. At least in this sector, I mean. We'd have made it in time, but thanks to your help—"

"Tell me how you did it, Wally," I said impatiently. "Our deadline is getting close."

"We had our people—few as they are—spread from here to hell and back along the border last night. Paid off. One of our teams spotted the truck down there not too far from where you do all your snipe hunting. Saw them make the pickup of wets and then they radioed our other units.

"We were in place, waiting for them at the barn. When they started to unload the illegals, we moved in." I looked over at Bran. He still looked puzzled. Mitch sat at his desk, the yellow copy pencil still in his hand, a slight smile on his face.

"No problems on the arrests," said the border patrolman. "We picked up twenty-three illegals, and one Jesus Perez and one Lawrence Rylow. We'd put the word out last night—Fred was on the phone even before you left headquarters—and Oklahoma State Police picked up the two trailers, the drivers and their loads of aliens somewhere between Oklahoma City and Tulsa." I closed my eyes for a second when Wally said that and I had to take a deep breath to keep from choking up. Poor Vicente.

"There apparently are other drivers working with the outfit," Wally was saying, "but we'll grab them in a day or two. As for the Mexican end of the operation—well, there's nothing we can do about that."

"Now, hold on a second, Wally," I said. "Let me catch up with you here in my notes." I scribbled fast as I could, trying to get it all down.

"Then Rylow is that *numero uno* you'd been telling me about?" I asked.

Wally shook his head. "Afraid not," he said softly. "The way it's looking it's. . . ."

Mitch's swivel chair squeaked. Someday he'd have to oil it.

"What Wally's trying to say," said Mitch, standing and walking to my desk, "is that I'm your *numero uno.*"

Mitch sat on the edge of my desk and I smiled up at him. "Come on now, Mitch—I'm trying to get this story for today's paper. Joke with me later, not now."

But then I saw in Mitch's face that he wasn't joking. His eyes were dark and there was sorrow in them, and what must've been regret. The smile remained on his face, but there was no humor in it.

Bran's face was white. He walked around his desk and dropped heavily into his chair. His hands were trembling and he put them in his lap. My heart fluttered and my breaths were short and I tried to say something, but couldn't. Swallowing hard, I looked up at Mitch. I didn't believe it. Mitch. Oh, God, my "uncle," my dad's best friend. The man who had saved my father's life in Korea. I felt a tear run down my cheek and I fought to keep from crying.

"I'm sorry, son," Mitch said, and he reached out a hand and tousled my hair. "I didn't mean to disappoint you like this. I'm going to tell you how it was, Matt, so you hear it from me. Get it all down, you'll need it for your story." Wally drew a small notebook from his pocket.

"Mitch," he said softly, "your rights. I've got to warn you that anything you—"

"I know, Wally," said Mitch, nodding. "It can all be held against me, but that doesn't matter right now. What's important is that Matt know the truth."

Turning to me, he let out a deep sigh.

"At first it was compassion, I suppose you'd call it," he began. "It was a chance to help some people, and God knows, they needed help. I've traveled plenty below the border and I know how it is down there.

"Well, at the start there were just a few of them. It was a lark, and it made me feel good, helping them. You know, I'd just get them across the border and that was it. They'd be on their own. But then it got out of hand and the money—well, the money started pouring in."

Sighing, Mitch looked down to stare at his fingernails, as if they could explain it all to him. "Well, Matt, you know how I feel about the newspaper business and about how I've itched to get away from it and live on the ranch? Well, here was my chance. I'd be able to help people and make piles of money while I was doing it."

Stunned, I sat in my chair, unable to move. I couldn't believe the words I was hearing. Not Mitch. Not my

Uncle Mitch. He was teasing me, and in just a minute he'd grin the way he does and say it was all a big joke. But he didn't grin, he didn't say it was a joke, and suddenly I felt my great little world tumbling down on top of me.

"Get this straight, Matt—I'm not making any excuses for what I did," he said. "All along I knew what I was getting into, what I was doing, and I went ahead knowing it was wrong. I knew full well that sometime I'd have to pay for it and—well, it appears that time has come."

For a second his eyes met mine, then he lowered them again to study his fingernails.

"Uncle Mitch—I'm sorry," I said. "I couldn't write this story. Not now, I couldn't. I had no idea you—"

" 'Course you didn't, Matt. You had no way of knowing. But I'm the one who messed up, not you. Greed does strange things to a man. I have no one to blame but myself. What you did was right, Matt, and you did it well. Remember that, please. There was nothing else you could do because you were a reporter after the facts, after the truth. Much as I personally dislike being in the newspaper business, I have nothing but the deepest respect for it.

"And I respect you, too, Matt, for breaking this story. Now you're bound by honor to write it, to put down the facts, to let the people know. It's your story and that's what this damned business is all about."

"Aunt Beth," I said almost to myself. "And Shan. . . ." Mitch didn't answer.

"*Dad!* Mitch, what's *Dad* going to say? You saved his

life—ever since I was a little kid I've been hearing about—about how he 'owes you one.' . . ."

"I'll call your father, Matt, and I'll tell him. It'll be easier for me. Far as I'm concerned, the account is paid in full. He doesn't 'owe me one' any longer. Sounds foolish now, I suppose, but some day you'll understand what I mean. I'm proud of you, Matt; I'm proud of what you've done. You're going to be one hell of a fine reporter. You have a gift, son, and it's a rare one. Use it wisely and use it well."

All at once the tears came. I just couldn't hold them back any longer. Mitch laid his arm on my shoulder and squeezed it. Clearing his throat, he said, "Enough of that, Matt. You've got a story to write, and Bran—if you'll take over the desk for me, I'd appreciate it."

My knees were weak and I didn't know if I could trust my legs, but I stood up and turned to Mitch. I hugged him, like I sometimes do my father when one of us is going away, and then Mitch shook my hand.

"Write it well, Winky," he said, softly, "write it well." Mitch's eyes were brimming with tears and he turned quickly from me and walked to the stairs. Wally lifted a hand, as if to say so long, and then he and Fred followed Mitch down the stairs.

Back at my desk I crossed my arms on the typewriter and put my head down. I still couldn't believe what had just happened. My head was spinning and surely I'd wake up and realize I'd just dreamed it all. I thought of Beth and Shan and I just wanted to die. What would Shannon say? What would she think? We loved each other. *Had* loved each other. But now nothing could ever be the same again. Not ever.

"Come on now, get with it, will you," Bran said, trying to sound gruff. He cleared his throat. "You've got a deadline staring you in the face. I want that story in my hands in forty minutes—we can't hold the press a minute longer than that."

I raised my head and looked at Trevor Brannigan. Somehow he looked older than he had an hour before. His eyes were filled with tears and he pulled out his handkerchief and blew his nose.

"Go on," he said. "If you don't write it the guys up in Tucson or Phoenix will get the story first, and for God's sake, you don't want them to break it, do you, Mark?"

I shook my head and told him I'd write it.

Rolling a sheet of copy paper into my old Underwood, I typed, "althaus, alien smugglers, p-1," and a few inches below that I began my story.

As I wrote the tears dropped onto the typewriter keys and onto my fingers.

25

BRAN HAD SAID he'd drive me up to Tucson that afternoon so I could catch a late flight back home. I just couldn't stay in Crandall another night. Twenty minutes before he was to pick me up at the Railroad Hotel, I had all my things down in the lobby and I was sitting in an old, overstuffed chair, waiting and thinking.

Then I realized there was something I had to buy. I asked the clerk to keep an eye on my bags while I ran over to a shop on Copper Avenue. I was back at the hotel in ten minutes and had my luggage piled at the curb by the time Bran pulled up. He opened the trunk of the Maverick and helped me load it. I climbed into the front seat, holding carefully in my lap what I had just bought.

"I have to stop at the Garritys' for just a minute, Bran," I said.

He looked at me over his glasses. "You sure?" he asked. He sounded surprised.

"I'm sure. There's something I have to do."

"You're the boss, Mark," he said, and he drove away from the curb.

"What happens now?" I asked him. "To Mitch, I mean."

"They took him up to Tucson this afternoon to make his initial appearance before the U. S. magistrate," Bran explained. "He'll be advised of his rights and of the charges against him. Bond will be set and he'll probably post it and be back here in Crandall tonight."

"And then?"

"Well, the matter will go to the federal grand jury in Tucson. The U. S. attorney will present his evidence to the jurors and they'll decide whether there's enough evidence against him. If there is, they'll hand down an indictment and then the magistrate will hold the arraignment. That's where Mitch will have his chance to enter a plea of guilty or not guilty."

"The trial comes next?"

"That's it—about thirty or forty days after the arraignment. Maybe more. There's always a lot of jockeying back and forth—a lot of delays."

"How do you think it'll come out?" I asked.

"You never know—plenty of evidence against him, the way it appears. But there's no way of predicting how a jury will act."

"If they find him—well, if he's guilty, what's the penalty?"

"Checked with an attorney friend this afternoon—wondered the same thing, myself." Bran paused. "Could be up to five years for each alien transported illegally." Five years!

"But that could add up to *hundreds* of years!" I said.

"It could, but it won't. They might charge him with one or two counts or let them run concurrently, and the judge might be feeling lenient and give him a lesser penalty, and then there's time off for good behavior—"

"But still, Bran, it could be years!"

"I'm sure Mitch knew that when he got himself involved in this mess. He knew the risks, Mark."

"Will you write to me? Will you let me know about the trial and all?" Bran said he would.

"One more thing you should know, Mark," said Bran. "Mitch had nothing to do with that beating you got last night. Sternaman told me Perez spotted my Maverick yesterday when he left the cattle-loading yard. He pulled the truck off the road and waited to see who was driving it. He stopped at the ranch then and set up the rough stuff with Larry Rylow. Mitch didn't know about it until after he was arrested, and he was furious when he found out."

Hearing that made me feel a lot better, even though I had known Mitch would never stand for anything like that.

"Bran—something else. Did you poke around my smuggling notes one night?"

"I'm guilty," he said, a sheepish smile on his lips. "Had a call from a friend on a paper in New York. He was doing a piece on undocumented aliens and needed some quick information. I knew you had it all together in those papers of yours and supposed I could put my hands on the details he needed faster that way than by going through the clipping file. Sorry—meant to tell you. It wasn't as if I was prying."

We pulled up in front of the Garritys' house then and I opened the car door.

"Only a couple of minutes," Bran said, looking at his wristwatch. "Jets don't wait."

"I might not even need a couple of minutes," I said. I realized then I didn't know what I would say, even if Shan would come to the door.

The front drapes were drawn and except for the cars in the carport, it looked as if no one was home. I knocked softly on the front door and waited, and then knocked again. The door opened a few inches, then slowly swung wider.

Shannon stepped outside and pulled the door closed behind her. Her eyes were red.

"You came," she said softly. "I didn't think you would."

"I didn't, either. Think I'd come, I mean." Seeing her, I felt as if I might cry again, and I didn't want to do that, so I bit my lip until I could taste blood. "I had to see you though, Shannie. I had to tell you good-bye and that I'm sorry. I didn't mean to hurt you—not ever."

She took a deep breath and nodded her head.

"It was a great summer, Shan. At least until today, it was."

She sniffed. "It was great," she whispered.

"You probably won't want to write to me now." She didn't answer. "I'll write first, Shan, and then if you feel like it, maybe you can. . . ." I let the sentence die in my mouth.

"I don't know, Matt. I mean, right now I just couldn't say."

"Sure," I said. And then I stood looking into her smokey gray eyes, hoping I could remember them as they had been before, full of mischief and joy, and not as they were now, clouded, and with tears in them.

I remembered then what I had bought up on Copper Avenue while I was waiting for Bran. I held the long box out to her and I watched as her fingers fumbled with it and then unwrapped the waxy green paper.

She lifted out the single pink sweetheart rose.

"They—they didn't have a yellow one," I apologized.

Shannon sucked in a deep ragged breath and squeezed her eyes tightly closed. When she opened them the tears rolled down both cheeks. She clutched the flower tightly.

And then Trevor Brannigan honked the Maverick's horn. I took a step backward and hesitantly she reached out one hand and with the tips of her long nails touched my arm.

"Winky," she said in a voice so tiny I could barely hear it. "Winky, Winky."

"I'm sorry, Shan," I whispered to her, and then I turned away and hurried to the car.